VOLUME 1

ANGELS FIGHTING DEMONS:

Visions Through The Binoculars of Revelation

D1600662

By Author

Milton Epting

Unless indicated, all Scripture are taken from the King James Version of the Holy Bible.

ANGELS FIGHTING DEMONS:

VISIONS THROUGH THE BINOCULARS OF REVELATION

This short story is a fictional literary work imparting some spiritual truths from the Kings James version of the Bible in a symbolic gesture. By no means does it represent any true direct statements of any religious doctrine. Some of this literary work is a personification of my imagination that grew out of past experiences and studies.

ISBN-13: 978-1732017900

Printed in the United States of America

In the loving remembrance of a praying grandmother, A.M. Cleveland.

Table of Contents

ANGELS FIGHTING DEMONS: Visions Through The Binoculars of Revelation

INTRODUCTION

Through the Binoculars of revelation, see the Wings of Wisdom fly High above the Heights of Ignorance. This book is a fantasy short story that stretches the imagination, crocheted and knitted in the tapestry of truth. Receive spiritual insight into the hidden kingdoms in the first, second, and third heavens, which is not a fairytale, but more real than the invisible air you are inhaling, and exhaling right now. The first heaven is the realm of the atmosphere where the eagles take flight with their powerful binocular vision, high above the majestic mountains. The mysterious second heaven is where Satan's invisible kingdom is established in outer space, where the sun, moon, stars, and galaxies are positioned below his army of darkness. The abode of God's throne is in the third heaven where the Lion of Judah sits on the right hand of the Most High, where angels are ascending, and descending upon his heavenly throne.

When the human eye receives light through its pupil, the perceived light rays are converted and transformed into an electrically generated signal that produces three dimensional images. The produced images are only part of the big picture that your eyes have generated. The unseen angelic world stands right in your midst in their invisible form everyday, but your natural eyes cannot see them. After being healed by a prophet from the Islands decades ago, my spiritual eyes were open by Elohim to witness angelic and demonic heavenly battles that revolutionized my life. There are countless invisible angelic battles taking place on all levels, right at this very moment while you are scanning these pages with your set of eyes.

I struggled with the thought of penning this book, because one day I desired to read on the subject, Angels fighting Demons, but I couldn't find it anywhere, which troubled me. After steadfast prayer, I decided to use my imagination, and life experiences to pen this fantasy short story saturated in some truths so that believers can relate to some of the episodes throughout the chapters. Creative angelic characters are flying and personifying themselves from page to page throughout this book, building heart thumping drama that will keep you on the edge of your seat, as you travel with them through each episode. Don't forget our imagination is a gift from the Most High which I maximize on a few pages throughout this story. This book is only a fraction of what I wanted to illustrate, but hopefully, down the road, we can meet again in another powerful episode. Through the Binoculars of Revelation, a narrating hidden angel witness angelic conflict and interaction, through his angelic eyes while peeping through a keyhole in a heavenly door. Listen to the angel tell the story by setting aside stereotypes, and preconceived notions that can cloud your judgement before you finish reading the last page, which could rob you of a positive opinion. The short story is told by him, predicated on what he saw through the door keyhole and his heavenly position as a guest angel standing on the wings of the wind.

The Kingdom of Darkness became obsessed with an intercessor because of something in his possession, which stirred the heavens. His faith, and deep devotion to the Most High brought divine intervention right to his front door. Be an eyewitness as the Good angels clash with the Evil bad angels over one anointed soul. The Third Heaven Angelic Air-force (the Most High angels) answered the bell in round one of this short story after being infuriated by the Satanic Flying Angels, who crossed a heavenly demilitarization zone and attacked a faithful heir of the Most High without receiving his permission. The heavens exploded as the Most High angels unleashed a vicious assault on the Kingdom of Darkness that sent an unforgettable message to their leaders forever.

These intelligent, powerful celestial beings set up platform altars in the four elements of fire, air, water, and earth, to unleash their destructive powers against humanity in retaliation against the Most High. They are scholars when it comes to understanding what the word of the Most High dictates to man. They know if they can get humanity to sin, then a spiritual door is open for one of their agents to bring an

evil reward to the violator. As they say at the movies,

"Warning: Viewer Discretion is advised." Enjoy the read!

ANGELS FIGHTING DEMONS

Angelic Attorneys in the Throne Room

As the dusty clouds of fire began to illuminate the ominous portals of the foggy black tunnels, the disembodied flying shadowy figures swirled upward from the dark energy in a spinning cycle of confusion. Screaming wild hysterical shrieks in the second heaven could be heard down below in the belly of the earth realm which could even make the ears of a deaf man want to wear earplugs. Something diabolical began to shift between two worlds of hidden mysteries with an immobilizing force as they yearned to satisfy their insatiable appetite, even though the air smelled like tombs of decaying flesh.

The sorcerous lightning flashed, streaking across the expansion of the cobra black sky with electrostatic crackling hellfire, charging the unforgiving lukewarm atmosphere. Suddenly the growling explosive thunder detonated in the second heaven, bursting the death-like fragile veil of eerie silence.

In the divine Throne Room located on the Northside up above in the third heaven, the Most High's throne, there was a historic gathering about to commence. It was ready to render its divine verdict on a court case brought before them by a Ruler of Darkness conspiracy against a particular person of interest under the first heaven. Behind two golden French Renaissance style giant doors, a court case was being appealed to the heavens. Through one of the doors key hole, a guest angel peeped through and witnessed some bone chilling action, and this is his story.

He saw a loathsome wicked archangel glowing with incredible intensity, blaring rumbling echoes of false allegations before the heavenly court. He was arguing about a cease fire divine decree approved by the Most High that was requested by a team of fervent intercessors, who were standing in the gap for a suicidal patient in a mental ward. Intercessors were men and women recognized as prayer warriors, who unselfishly prayed for the human race, nations, and almost anything that needed divine intervention, and salvation. These spiritual intercessors in the earth realm would petition the 3rd Heaven at a set time of prayer every week. Demonic infusions of evil thoughts were downloading to the suicidal patient's mind like wicked movies from a satellite signal that was almost unbearable. This was one of the cases the Dark Shadow Legal team was trying to get reverse so they could finish destroying their target, but a heavenly issued restraining order was blocking them. With a misinformation campaign in mind, the evil angel with lightning discharging back and forth over his glowing red eyes began to spew out a flood of convincing lie's trying to destabilize the Throne Room. Suddenly there was an ear deafening bellow that jammed all demonic frequencies in the gravitational soundwaves as a shocking quiescence garbed the courtroom with an awful hush.

"Objection your Honor!" Then a supreme voice superior over all voices in the world, spoke with authority saying, "Objection sustain!" His words echoed, reverberating seven times like a loud clap of thunder cleansing the soundwaves of the room's chamber that was contaminated by the howling flickering energy from the evil angel's crooked mouth. Suddenly the forces of darkness fell to the floor as dead men hit with angel fire, with their hands covering their bulging eyes trembling, and shaking in bewilderment. Their tactics were not permissible in the Throne Room court, so they paid a steep price for the illegal approach. With a wheezing spine-chilling voice as haunting as a burial chamber, the Demonic Prosecuting Attorney stood up, raised and flapped his humongous celestial wings to regain his composure. He sighed, and mumbled under his breath, stuttering, "We rest our case." As eerie tranquility sheathed the courtroom, the Dark Shadow Legal staff knew they hadn't proved their case, so they conceded after hearing the ancient, eternal voice of the Most High, the presiding Judge, intervene on behalf of the intercessors. No cross examination was necessary in their case. Dark Shadow was an evil invisible law firm created and formed by the kingdom of darkness to represent appealed cases in the heavens. There were several more cases on the court docket for the day, but the one that had the kingdom of darkness gossiping was soon to come. Then a Bailiff angel, deputized by the Most High, cried out saying, "Who is next"?

Saipon, the angelic prosecuting attorney of the Dark Shadows, was disturbed as he moved his whip like reptilian tail playfully behind his diabolical body with movement reminiscent of a stalking cat. Outside the Throne Room, a winged symphony of heavenly angels were rehearsing, preparing for an uplifting praise song for the Most High while cylinders of lights seep through the expansion of the heavens like revolving stage lights.

With overpowering animosity, Saipon stared at the enticing portals above the galaxies with his piercing red eyes burning with rage, as infernal lights escaped the quadruple rows of outlets surrounding his wolf-like nostrils where hairy, slimy maggots crawled in delightful glee. Jagged bones thrusted out of his sinewy, muscular body, while broken thick rusty chains stuck in his flesh hidden under his fiery feathers from an old abyss jail break escapade. When he snarled, you could see his copper fanged mandibles protruding from his face gleaming in sparkling twilights as toxic smog escaped his draconic nostrils from his imposing Neanderthal Goliath stature. With bushy boney brows, he also argued and litigated in court against an illegal spiritual warfare session fought in the heavens by a prayer warrior name Sid who lives in the physical realm, earth. After giving his bellowing deposition, he took flight with a burst of enchanting energy lifting his robust body, darting with glee to his vacant seat at the throne room conference table hissing with his reptilian slithery fork tongue mocking the Angelic Defense team.

The ceiling in the Throne Room sparkled and flickered with a scintillating Zion like fire with escaping chords of bedazzling soft lights cascading and shimmering across the room calming the dark shadowy energy. A throne room perspective fragrance filled the room with an aroma of victory soon to come for the winning legal team.

The invisible kingdom called the third heaven was adjudicating an executive order against the second heaven constituents, to determine whether diplomatic kingdom immunity could be granted to an anonymous earthly exorcist in a court case the kingdom of darkness opposed. The exorcist had trodden and chartered satanic territories in the south border of a small town called Ishkooda in the state of Alabama, where poltergeist white misty stardust lingered in the air detecting his presence. The white stardust was better known as hissing hot devil spit amongst the ranks of the disembodied foot soldiers of darkness who laid the snare. Once a violator passed through the mist, the satanic trap contaminated him, which is known as spiritual marking in the hidden empire of darkness that gives allegiance to Satan. In this court case, the exorcist forgot to enforce his decrees in the Most High name to cleanse the four elements to prevent spiritual marking for demonic surveillance. The four elements, fire, water, wind, and earth, needed cleansing with a Godly DNA, better known as the blood of the Son of the Most High. Therefore, he unknowingly triggered the hellhound sirens for a satanic attack decreasing his chances of completing his undercover assignment. Sid was a dedicated holy intercessor for the human race who was unaware of demonic tracking devices. He prayed for deliverance for the nation daily. His effectual fervent prayers would summon warrior angels into unseen heavenly battles approved by the Most High. His ministry spiritual thermometer temp was never lukewarm but always hot. There was also something in Sid's possession the evil empire had a deep interest, stored away in his house. He purchased something from an anonymous vendor that would eventually turn his world upside down. The purchase didn't go unnoticed by the devils. They always magnified anything he did.

Vertically above the earth realm, in a clamor of rumbling darkness, jangling chains broke the silence in the 2nd Heaven. Two fanged mouth rogue demonic angels with thick shoulder length manes, escaped quickly in the dark portal, from angelic custody as the barbecue red moon appeared like a dragon-flame disc in the sensual Shulamite sky. Harp strings of moonlight lasered across the surface of the mystical rivers below like lines of glittering fire, in the tranquil serene valley. The cumbering river coiled like a serpent through the deciduous forest, spray dancing over glossy rocks while fleeting spotted garfish zigzagged, and raced through the rippling crystal blue currents. There were two college lovers dressed alike horseback riding while their assigned angels sent by the Most High stood on guard like alert law enforcement agents. They were perched on the giant smooth grey boulders above the graceful flowing waterfall watching all of their movement in the sacred valley. Most of the human population was unaware of the heavenly court, and Throne Room in the third heaven.

The onyx black condemned sky in the second heaven was moaning, and groaning like the upset stomach of an angry barbarian god, because someone on earth was fighting them with spiritual warfare. As the snarling wind howled, above the pregnant malicious fire-worshipping clouds, putrefying and decomposing fleshy air, flooded the atmosphere in Lucifer's headquarters in the second heaven. The Second heaven is where the hidden empire of darkness rendered dark worship before him night and day, on the vulcanite black altar of death,

with mind channeling whispers of dark praise.

Prayer Fuels the Battles

An invisible telecommunication network channeling tower hidden in a deep layered dark portal of the second heaven, received an emergency satanic Wi-Fi signal from demonic forces under exploding gamma rays for immediate attention. Permission was granted by cosmic creatures in the second heaven to begin harassment operations against a certain target of interest, Sid. These malevolent angelic beasts were cannibalistic soul hunters that pierced the darkness between the portals of the nether world. The dark shadows studied their enemy's religion so they could receive legal access to attack when one of them succumb to temptation. They would also appeal to the Most High in the Throne Room for permission to attack when believers walked out of fellowship with him because of depravity. These atrocious fiends were divine attorneys that knew about all the laws of heaven like seasoned United Nation attorneys.

Then a scorching bolt of white lightning suddenly flashed under the collapsing summer sky, frothing with furious intensity. Under the first heaven, something eerie foreboding, and mysterious was looming in the spiritual realm. Veiled in a swirling warlock wind of Barabbas blackness, was a squint-eyed grimacing Centauroid goat headed angel with silver fangs protruding from his mouth. He was airborne over Sid's neighborhood, defying gravity with a bellowing howl in dark shadows. The creature was gasping for breath through his gnarled constricting nostrils, oozing copious mucus snot infused with demonic fluids, trickling down his obsidian neutered humanoid body. He appeared to be in twisted agony as his jugular neck vein swirled with snake like movements under three layers of transmutated bark thick skin that persistently fizzled and pop. The demon was fighting against tormenting excruciating pain, to regurgitate slimy and cocoon shaped hairy eggs, he swallowed delightfully in his pregnant miscarrying belly, protruding above his biped feet. Suddenly chaotic energy escaped the enchanting darkness, whistling through the sprawling trees, rustling the crackling leaves on snapping branches, while gripping huge roots spread eagle the trembling curse ground, twisting toward bowel loosening devilish depths, like a giant squid devouring his virgin prey. Surging from his blubbery elongated mouth, a violent eruption of hot amniotic tangy fluid, exploded from his constricting throat. Then an ascending swarm of jade-green Beelzebub armored fighting flies, rose high in the boundless sky emanating a mordant perfume of emaciated decaying cadavers. The suffocating stench even made the foul-smelling demons frown and gasped for air. The bloodsucking sickly disease carrying flies, bombed dive like Japanese kamikaze warplanes near Sid's house from infinity hidden portals, with deep layers of terror, where sweltering heat, and vision suffocating darkness, hid the secret pit of the Abyss, the forbidden realm.

They were satanically programmed to reach their destination in about thirteen minutes. The number thirteen, was significant to them because it represented rebellion and lawlessness. The Nimrod satanic calendar up in the second heaven had this particular day circled, because of a violation Sid had committed. But the third heaven hadn't granted any permission to the kingdom of darkness to attack because the case was still pending in the heavenly courts.

Spiritual gang banging in a termite bonded log cabin located in the dark woods, where sycamore trees, and tall stalks of sugar cane, grew beyond their unkempt boundaries on the west-side of town, was about to go down. As a gust of wind blew through the silhouette of the shady trees, in the early morning hours, the sun was grilling a little-isolated town like an overcook kosher hotdog called Ishkooda. It was a playground for wild knuckle walking creatures that drove the town mad at night, where serenity was ruptured with a raucous cry by shrieking voices when there was a full moon.

Sid, a devout young man who feared the Most High, opened a tattered torn book and read a logos scripture that leaped off the page of the spiritually discerned manuscript. It was full of highlights of inheritance rights reserved for its heirs and joint-heirs through a process called faith. This book was no fairy tale or science fiction novel, but it contained rhema living words that Sid conditioned his life around over the last seven years. The letters KJV had worn away from the front of the bookbinder because of his mindboggling studying habits. Usually, a tapestry of silence and beauty impregnated the molecular edifice of his cozy home deep in the belly of the dark woods.

A couple of days ago he sprayed foam pesticide feverishly around the flooring in his basement after seeing aggressive fire ants committing a home invasion on his property. He also would play anointed music by internet inside his house each day to keep tiptoeing bulbous jaundice eyed demons away. The music frequency and chord tones were saturated with the Spirit of the Most High which tormented and roasted trespassing demons.

One evening soaring high in the gloomy clouds, a dark gargantuan-piercing eyed demon with a vestigial scythe like tail that glowed like red embers, was on satanic assignment. He was stirring up a dark thunderstorm while he was in flight with his enormous, powerful wings unfurled over Sid's neighborhood, so he could sabotage Sid's electrical power in his home by tossing wicked lightning strikes at the power lines. The thick curly tail bulging face demon with dark smoking satanic symbols branded on his torso, short-circuit the electrical power in Sid's house so his anointed internet music generated by AC power would stop playing. Then flightless speedy demonic foot soldiers would peep through his window for reconnaissance operations for future attacks.

Suddenly, there was a scratching noise coming from under his house, penetrating his hardwood floors. He took a long calculating look at the floor, choking from secreted saliva gurgling in his mouth. He said, "That can't be rats I am hearing." With botox puffy cheeks, and his baby blue eyes bulging from their sockets, he was slumped with graceful exhaustion lying on his chocolate leather sofa. He quickly sat up like an intoxicated jack in a box, kicking off his imported leopard skin shoes. With a lockdown gaze staring at the floor, he froze like a stalking immobilized jaguar, listening closely to descramble the mysterious sound. Sid could sense something malicious was stalking him. Subliminally he could smell an ungodly battle getting ready to be unleashed. He tiptoed across the cold cracking hardwood floors, and peeped out his kitchen bay window, tilting his venetian blinds with his fingers, but he saw nothing but his nosey neighbor sweeping his front porch. Then like a crashing resounding cymbal bang, there was an ear-splitting clap of thunder. Finally, it happens!

There was an imminent breach in his hedge of protection. His supernatural radar system, a multitude of invisible Warrior Angels, identified enemy forces violating Sid's airspace. A dark horde of green infested satanic flies humming like buzzing chainsaws began to rivet against his house from the north, south, east, and west. They descended like an unholy plague of hell-born death machines with four ghastly glaring eyes staring through his soul with paralyzing ferocity in the sparkling night energy. Then it dawned on him that he was under attack by evil spirits. Like silver bullets ricocheting off titanium steel doors, the green beady-eyed galactically created flies inseminated with angel DNA, bounced and somersaulted back into the Windstream above his house out of control. The demonic invasion transpired because Sid had decreed powerful scriptures the night before from his book of faith. He would always decree a thousand shall fall on his side and ten thousand on his right-hand side. Sid knew his spiritual rights like a cop reciting Miranda rights from memory.

Then counterattacking thoughts consumed his conscious. He shouted, "Let a firewall surround my home now!" Suddenly his guardian Angel dressed in a linen priestly robe sprinted like a speed merchant exploding from his starting blocks in a one hundred yard dash morphing himself into a wall of inferno fire. He orbited the log cabin home seven thousand times in a millisecond running ten thousand times faster than the human eye can blink, generating heat as hot as the breath of Satan fulfilling Sid's commandment. He began to engage in spiritual warfare prayer by requesting that all hidden evil spirits be revealed in the 3rd Heaven light of the Most High.

The battle started. Sid yelled loudly from his belly, "So you want to steal, kill, and destroy huh," while looking all around the room like a lost child searching for his mother! Then suddenly the howling wind outside shifted to demon speed with the smell of an ungodly odor hanging in the air. Sid went into a shut-in closing himself in his home from the outside world, then he began to sing and pray unto the Most High. He decreed, "I strip, disarm, and bind every devil that has taken on the form of invisibility. You are loosed and dismissed from your assignments. I strike you all with blindness, dumbness, and deafness in the Almighty name of the Most High. I jam your satanic frequencies. I cancel out this attack and arrest this satanic activity. I call and deploy giant warrior angels for divine assistance to help fight this battle on my behalf. You devils are commanded to decommission yourself from your task and place over my domain in the name of the Most High." The words Sid spoke was recorded and archived by an unseen Musicologist Angel that was responsible for retaining sounds waves, frequencies, and vibrations created from words spoken from a believer's pure heart. This Angel had oscillating praise and golden worship cylinder pipes along with digital signal processing strings assembled in his back that ran from behind his neck down his celestial spine like a guitar. When he flaps his harp like musical wings that emulated the sound of a guitar, the frequencies of Sid's words were harmoniously transferred with blinding light speed directly to the ears of the Most High for divine intervention. In less than one fraction of a second, Sid was alerted by his guardian angel that his request for divine intervention was granted by the Heavens. It was said before he call the Most High, he had already answered. As the Angel was flying away to his next assignment, Sid heard his flapping musical wings playing the chords to a song called "Don't wait till the battle is over you can shout now."

Suddenly, after a bawling howl in the nebula signaling all tar black shadows. A train of Shekinah heavenly glory swirled with a divine electroluminescent light shimmering off the descending scattering dark clouds. It started forcing the infrared laser funneling wicked spirits backwards, forming a trail of thread-like smoke with a feverish energy as the bowels of darkness craved for angelic flesh to satisfy its hunger. They couldn't see their subject, Sid, with their night vision encapsulated eyes because blindness struck them as Sid prayed.

The 3rd Heaven Angels were infuriated with their adversaries, after receiving fighting orders triggered by Sid's warfare prayer, and a heated battle ensued, to enforce the decrees and declarations. Seething with divine anger, the Most High angels departed from their secret dimension, and crossover through the dark triple layered portal, as their majestic wings caught the air, they took the second heaven airwaves, thirsty for a bloodbath battle with wings sounding like thousands of rushing chariots, fueled with a Zion energy. They were anointed to slaughter, and take no hostages that were commanded from the lips of righteous prayer. Dangerous prayers stirred up dangerous battles.

Angel fire showered the turbulent sky in the second heaven, blasting and flinging devil DNA genes like a confetti parade. The Most High angels had arrived, fuming with anger.

They were swinging their flaming swords desperately with all their divine strength, increasing the intensity of the fierce battle. It was the sight of a pure eerie nightmare, setting the stage for a full blown invisible invasion, as the cosmic beasts of the nebula were unleash with wild animal hatred in their menacing eyes. The more evil the dark shadows consume in their immoral minds mysteriously sharpen their fangs and claws while their blasphemous wings grew stronger as the violence rage on. Spineless flying dark angels were dodging death blows with dragonfly-like quickness while the lower level dark celestial angels with mauling fangs, were being sliced and flayed, as the Angels slashed through the ranks of Satan's battalions. In forlorn hope, the chasmal mouth ram headed armored devils were no match for the Most High battle tested Angelic Air-force (the Most High Angels).

Swords were clanking in darkness, as the vile effluvium smell of death surrounded the battlefield. The saline taste of angelic blood sprinkled on demonic tongues, excited their subliminal conscious. A legion of flying devils stomped their feet on top of the ember red renegade shooting meteorites, triggering

explosions, bringing them delightful glee. They roared

blasphemous epithets at the descending heavenly angels,

soaring from the multicolored rings of Saturn.

The arctic cold howling wind keened, and mewled down,

penetrating to the depths of their angelic soul, as they ghastly

stared disdainfully with angry curled trembling upper lips. The

stare down face to face in the nebula, sent rushing secreted

adrenaline, as raging fire in their divine bodies. As shreds of

phantasm grey mist divided both parties, there instantly was

rumbling thunder. The troll bulging face demons with writhing

tentacles covering their whole body, rushed forward with a

bellowing cry, like a black plague of devouring cryptic beasts,

as their marauding wings lacerated the air. The abysmal

charging demons crashed their swords against the angel's

indestructible shields, knocking them almost unconsciously off

balance, causing them to collide with their galloping squealing

and screaming horses. The soaring warrior angels quickly

recovered, but before they could unsheathe their mighty

swords strapped tightly on their sides, the powerful blood thirsty devils jumped them again and continued to slam their swords, over and over with deadly intent, pounding and pummeling them repetitively, forcing them to keep both hands on their shields. Their secret strategy was to force the angels, to keep both hands on their shields, and away from their 3rd heaven deadly swords; then the demons planned to signal hidden cannibalistic devils, bunkered below in the layered portal, to ambush them all. With disheartening somber, lurking over the battle with eerie foreboding. The warrior angels under attack, spoke in an unknown mysterious tongue talking to each other, which confused the devils, but they continue to forcefully thrash the angel's shields nonstop, to keep their hands off those swords. After communing under intense outside pressure, the calm angels came up with a plan, to intensify the brightness of their bodies, to blind the devils, then liberate and vindicate themselves. All at once without any warning, the angels unfurled their wings, and their bodies bursted forth into Shekinah glory mode, shining with the luminosity of a billion suns, blinding the ghastly three eyed monsters.

Suddenly there were slithering sounds of thousands of swords being unsheathed.

It was too late for the nervous devils to repent. Bawling echoes of screaming, and yowling, escaped the rigid demonic mouths of the blinded beasts, as carnage, and fountains of blood showered into the air. The flood of monstrous beasts that broke their lines, who worshipped darkness rather than light, cursed the angels with their blood soaked faces, and sunken eyes filled with blasphemy. The battle tested angels had sliced and thrusted through the solar plexus of the dark beasts with their swords, as the acrid smell of blood rose up in their mouths. You could hear the snarling, growling, and the flesh tearing screams traveling in the electromagnetic waves, as the Most High angels surge forward to the center of the intense fighting. Silver fire winged Seraphim angels were free falling from high altitudes through the constellations in the second heaven like a hail storm, barrel rolling their glistening bodies like war aircraft in a downward spiral as if they were wounded trying to bait more evil forces into the battle. Anxious glowing gold haired angels with tight face concentration and built-in radar were flying intentionally upside down like an intoxicated aviator, scanning the darkness for the intruders, hoping the aggressive evil angels would engage them from their Beelzebub hideouts. The heavenly battleground in the second heaven was like a pyrotechnic show with satanic anointed butchered bowels squirting and spraying slippery celestial fluid like a tropical storm. Wounded cosmic dark creatures were wailing and screaming hysterically, after seeing their mangled spiky bone bodies from a mirror like reflecting North Star. The lightning quick Angels warring for Sid were determined to torture all trespassers that crossed territorial latitudinal lines with no permission granted by the Most High in the veil of darkness.

They were too quick, too powerful, and three times deadlier than their adversaries. With wandering eyes searching their surroundings, a battalion of fast approaching powerful angels roared in flight with so much G-Force in the heavens, until the Ishkoodians felt the rumbling and thundering vibrating on the cold ground floor under their feet. All of these warriors were immune to human weapons. For they were created from the clandestine Heavenly Treasury Chest of top-secret Lights, and Hidden classified secrets that belong to the Most High.

In midair, a somersaulting sparkling warrior angel backhanded and drop kicked a fast approaching legion of flying devils that caused them to lose conscious falling motionlessly like someone hit by the straight fist of a god. Earlier a taurine molten red devil with terror hiding inside his heart swung an enchanting razor sharp sword at the angel, and almost decapitated him. Swarms of roaring chain armored sphinx headed evil angels rose from spiraling black bottomless pools darkening the face of the moon with outstretch dark wings beating against the air generating electrical windstorms. The scorching hot wind, as hot as Greek fire, was whipping against the face of the angels as their voices echoed with hostility and brutality. Glowing-gold moonlight was gleaming down on the second heaven, increasing the battle fever, while the fire breasted devils surged forward to relieve their angelic alpha warriors on the front line who were being assaulted by the swarming 3rd Heaven Angels. Three ghastly red eyed demonic beasts riding on galloping lion face centaur stallions, breathing dragon fire from their wolf like nostrils, joined their arms together and clotheslined a heavenly warrior Angel, who was riding his divine horses and chariots of fire with light speed right beneath them that flipped him backwards into a deep crater on Jupiter, damaging his wings. Rivers of pulsating heavenly spilled lights were reflecting off the slashing, and shiny double bladed swords creating a three dimensional strobe light effect on the gravitational battleground, not far from Saturn. These angels granted no mercy.

Hidden behind an elite regiment of special operation forces, was a cobalt eyed, ten foot tall lion-like devil standing majestically shaking space fleas from his swirling gold hair mane in the spellbound wind with bulging varicose veins percolating under his skin. He was riding a six dimensional spinning wheel chariot, pulled by six stygian black stallions with sickle like claws treading forward swiftly with muscular tails slithering behind them. Speaking in a rushing tone with his pterodactyl tight skinned wingspan, he barked out orders to two rawboned imp thin flightless demons that rode his back pony style in heavenly battles wielding a bright sword.

He knew if he could distract Sid from praying, then the Most High flying army would yield to them until they receive new fighting orders from Sid. He planned to escape once Sid stop praying, and the battle halts. He motioned his wicked fingers in a secret sign language at the two gifted elf like imps that could make it rain hail with secret enchantments. These gelid eyed chiseled jaw demons could transmit strong, deceptive thoughts through the mind of mankind tricking them to believe the entertaining thought was from their God. The secret encrypted code behind his sign language was to have the imps to channel the mind of a lukewarm church member of Sid's. When the manipulated church member called Sid on his smart phone, it lured him off his knees to get up and answer his phone on the kitchen table. The kingdom of darkness had a secret hidden sign language that all devils memorize before getting involved in heavenly conflicts. This hidden demonic code was created to mock many prayer warriors because they didn't know their tongues could determine the outcome of certain heavenly battles. The demonic world knew prayer was the fuel for the Most High fighting army today. The mind channeling was working because Sid's smart phone started ringing. He had one eye tightly shut, and the other one open, glancing at his caller ID, while still praying in the spirit. Unfortunately, he disconnected spiritually from the heavens yielding to his flesh because of the suspenseful channeling thoughts enchanting his mind. He stopped praying and answered his smart phone. Suddenly in the second heaven, the swishes and hisses of powerful swords slashing through the gravitational air waves desisted, creating a cease fire atmosphere in the perilous battle. Up in the ghost grey sky of the heavens, the Most High Angelic Air-force, simultaneously put away their swords in their sheath waiting for their next assignment. If these angels were not provoked, then the enemy forces were free to go. Demons would tremble when angels remove their sword from their sheath because the sword was divinely created with secret supernatural powers to bring destruction to the Kingdom of darkness. When an angel swung his sword, a Shekinah glory of fire lit up the sky with dazzling energy release to burn demon flesh. Their blood, flesh, hair, and bones were created from mixtures of lights. Battles would occur within so many squares of sheet of lights because of territorial rights. The 3rd Heaven Air-Force had reclaimed the sky, and victory temporarily was Sid's.

With his raised Baphomet fist signifying demonic solidarity, and unification, the Lion hairy mane pointed ear devil with two ivory ram horns adorning his head began to roll his neck and shoulders while turning his chariot slow motion, signaling to all his evil angels to return back into the hidden black portal with a secret passage to a dual portal, after seeing the battle had halted. The diabolic wind was caressing his emaciated face and ruffling his unkempt hairy mane. With a crash in the darkness, they all escaped along with their wounded behind a giant nebula cloud of molecular gas concealing their departure. The heavenly battleground was littered with mutilated bodies, variegated bowels, and gory carnage in the gaslight bloodbath (invisible lights and gases escaping angelic entrails). The immortal evil agents immediately received a satanic recovery anointing that was applied to their wounds like the witch doctors do in the physical realm to heal their people, before the space gnats attack the putrid smelling wounds, causing stalactite, and dripping stalagmite formations on their celestial bodies. The vicious insect world in the second heaven was undiscovered and invisible to the 20/20 vision of the inhabitants down below in the earth realm. This heavenly battle was not visible to the human eyes even though both parties agreed to fight in the human form.

The rest of the evil angels had withdrawn back into the spiritual realm because Sid was still on the phone listening to the mind manipulated church member talking about the results of the Olympics' boxing match last night. One trick that seem to always succeed is the evil vehicle of delivery, when a believer is manipulated and not aware they are performing work for the kingdom of darkness. This battle was not a spiritual night dream, or some drug oriented hallucinated vision by Sid. But after long hours of praying, and bathing his soul in the sweet spirit of the Most High, these were visions of sudden releases of warfare power in the spiritual realm that summoned warrior angels. This warfare power sent confusion into the satanic radar network of the Kingdom of Darkness. Then shrieks, and petrified screams of horror like a woman in painful labor with child, reverberated in the second heaven which triggered the Principality to alert the district Ruler of Darkness for divine assistance. (The Principality didn't think his fleeing forces would survive after seeing the host of angelic armies fighting viciously in the battle for Sid.) Fighting in the earth domain with a human body was the most common battle approved by the 3rd Heaven. Illegalities and technicalities were scrutinized to the third degree because the earth was man's domain.

Demon-Freeze Allegiance to Darfur

"Send Demon-Freeze to my chambers as soon as possible," barked Darfur to his subordinates, while thrusting out his bulging chest in anticipation! He was questioning the fighting strategies of the Kingdom of Darkness angelic forces. He was one of mighty authority who would constantly grunt when stress overwhelms him. "I ordered them to fly and fight viciously with their backs toward the Sun," he said to himself in a reasoning tone. "When they engage in air to air combat from the North, then the sagacious enemy from the third heaven can't see us because of the blinding Sun and bright constellations." This was a figment of his imagination because the 3rd Heaven angels could stare face to face at the Sun without blinking for hours when they were monitoring fleeing Wicked Spirits in High Places. "Should I be concern about the gravitational force that's not affecting the torque of their wings," he shouted? "I demand an immediate answer," shouted Darfur at his subordinates! No one said a word because they knew he constantly talked to himself after battles, so they left him wrapped in his own dejection. He would throw tantrums, fits of rage, and yell obscenities when he read the weekly statistical report concerning warfare casualties after slurping and sipping a hot cup of soupy human blood with his long purple tongue in the morning hours. Solid clotted blood dissected from old cadavers was use like tea bags drop in satanically scalding hot water to satisfy his yearning for his favorite demon brew.

The 3rd Heaven Angels exploited the magnetic fields showing no signs of body friction when they propelled upward vertically flying thousands of miles, in self-defensive positions with flaming double edge swords. Wind and air were not necessary for these superior fighting angels from the third heaven to navigate and maneuver in flight. The rules of engagement for the heavenly battle was initiated by the second heaven Transylvania dark angels whose wicked bodies was half dark, and half molten red, with grids of psychedelic led lights embedded in their quads that emitted Morse codes when they flew signaling intelligence to ground forces. They communicated with sparkling blinking lights. Their sanctuary were gaping pits in dark craters where their obsidian skin would automatically change colors to match their environment. They paid a pernicious price for confronting their opponents in the human fighting mode where they transformed their celestial bodies, morphing into human DNA. There were numerous different fighting modes that were available to them, but the commanding captain of the Black-Z-Force regiment overruled Darfur's order and commanded all angels to go human mode. The flying gangsters could have chosen their invisible fighting mode which would have allowed the triple six lasers and dangerous sheets of lights to be use but their tactics backfired because the Most High angels had to engage in the human mode too because it was part of the second heaven agreement approved by the Most High in this domain battle. But they still were no match for the Most High Superior Angels. Darfur mind was cycling through options on what to do next to auspicious Sid, while he stared off into the constellations with a blasphemous evil desire. "I will not be disrespected, and allow insubordination to go unpunished in the heat of the heavenly battles, so we will talk about court martialing later when the eclipse has passed."

Then he looked at a mirror like star admiring his nightmarish amphibian red unblinking eyes gleaming with hatred and a hideous long sticky slithery tongue which squirmed and coiled within his powerful yawning mandibles protruding from his face. Hairs of flaming fire adorned his head with stubby black horns jutting from his bulging forehead, and ivory ram horns curled to the side of his head. He walked like a human but stalked like a feral eyed predator with powerful arms, and legs covered in ethereal reptilian flea crawling skin. Serrated sharp spike like growths ran down his spine that could be seen from the eyes of the clouds when he stretch his demonic wings in flight leaving a glowing amber fire in the air from each wing stroke. His divine purpose was to fulfill all of Satan's evil pessimistic plans in the earth realm. Darfur is a chilling Ruler of Darkness angel in the second heaven that's responsible for influencing spiritual territory below the atmosphere where Sid lives, which is locally called Ishkooda with a population of three thousand. He is ranked as a five-star general in the military structure of the evil spiritual empire with three thousand legions of demonic foot soldiers under his authority. These demons were satanically anointed to target and stop Judeo-Christian churches from praying. They always reported to Darfur so they could receive their weekly assignment through demonic frequencies on a normal basis. When it came to his attention a church was praying and fasting, he would take it personally. He would send infirmity demons and strong delusions of delicious fancy foods to their minds to urge them back to their irresistible refrigerators or drive through burger joints that tempted them to cheat doing the fast, and lie to their pastors which short circuited the flowing power from the Most High. Darfur spiritual, intellectual staff satanically influenced the local and city governments on a monthly basis which blocked blues laws and kept the liquor stores open seven days a week in Ishkooda. They would play a major role in city ordinances which impacted the morality of the county population. Whoever was assigned an angel by the Most High in the small town was also assigned a demon by the Kingdom of darkness. His surveillance of the enemy forces, which are active praying believers over the last five years brought him national recognition from Satan's invisible confidantes. He increased teenage drug addiction and murders by a whopping fifty percent in Ishkooda in less than six months. This small town also had one of the highest percentages of alcoholics in rehab than any town in the southwest because of demonic oppression.

Then a flash of lightning, a shriek resonating within dark thick clouds, suddenly a hulking obsidian tight skinned imposing beast with his massive torso surrounded in coils of toxic smoke encircling his diabolical body dipped in embers and fire, was staring with three eyes burning with a rage of ultraviolet debilitative severity. His head was adorned with shadowy bones and cracked skin, where infernal rays of lights escaped the surface liberating foul spirits dancing in the smelly fumes of decaying maggot infested flesh. Intense Gomorrah heat escaped his skewed nostrils within a fiery broad nose, breathing in frightening energy. He growled a thunderous bellow, surging with a roaring echo from his tusked mouth in furious defiance. There in absolute darkness, he bolted forward moving sluggishly, his four thick ebon leathery skin legs lumbering, carrying his cursed body with menacing dark energy. The unleash dark beast with a burning angels sword still plunge deeply in his sinewy back was crunching and masticating on flesh and bones of the dead as he soared bathing himself in the infrared, ultraviolet burning lights with colossal wings in the second heaven right below Darfur's headquarter. This was one of Darfur's Dark Warrior angels with an abysmal surprise, feeding on the dead that was snatched from a grave yard funeral before the body was buried.

"Have anybody seen Demon-Freeze and her posse'," whispered Darfur to his closest associate while rubbing his hands together like a slick street salesman? His associate is Rakeem, the shapeshifting angel from the undiscovered secret network of hidden planets in the second heaven. With his chiseled double chin resting in his sinister hands while sitting wide legged on a stack of Nephilim skulls, he was listening to soothing satanic iTunes lyrics through his dark skull-headphones, nodding his head to the groovy beat and wicked bass line.

"Ah yes, I know exactly where Demon-Freeze is," said the transfiguring devil with a look of fierceness and pride. Demon-Freeze, with electric energies pulsating from her body when she walks, is a multidimensional demon that teleported in the airwaves, accelerating between the first and second heavenly portals, wearing a long linen leopard print Miami vice gothic robe, concealing her secret weapons. Hidden under her intimidating flaming wings were vials of secret potions that she would pour in the clouds over a rebellious populated area to alter human behavior.   People would either murder, lust, steal, cheat, or rebel depending on which vial she drop on them. She also had crystal eyes that sparkle like diamonds and shiny gold fangs jutting from her mouth. Her name was given to her by a team of 3rd Heaven invisible archangels that arrested and caged her from a church concert at a dome designed tabernacle, where she was stalking the pastor's wife but an alert prophet nicknamed Eagle Eyes saw her in the spirit and screamed, "Demon Freeze, In the name of the Lord"! When the prophet said, "Be arrested and banned from this place by Angels, in the name of the Most High," the Warrior Angels quickly apprehended her, calling her Demon-Freeze before they uncage and release her in dry places unknown to the GPS in space.

"What's her plan this time," he said in a voice rippling with seductive overtones"? Rakeem, being driven by his obscure demonic impulse and narcissistic personality began to grin showing all his canine fangs like an underfed wolf. Then with a twisted delightful smile, he began to speak reluctantly saying, "Demon-Freeze is trying to get the upper hand on the new pastor's daughter who was admitted to Angel-Wings Psychiatric Hospital for repetitively fighting her children and constantly talking to herself." "She is mind channeling the psychiatric ward at the hospital over the mountain west of Ishkooda by opening a dimensional doorway in the second heaven so wicked frequencies can be downloaded to her mind when the full moon is in its strongest gravitating state," whispered Rakeem. "We targeted her for future satanic attacks, so the generational bloodline curse can continue in their dysfunctional family where multiple nights have ended in disasters because of her monstrous energy we downloaded. We have legal rights to channel our dark energy through her mind so we can block her identity with our many personalities. When her mother was pregnant with her, we use trauma in her marriage as a legal doorway to enter in the womb to afflict the embryo, and then we modified her DNA installed by the Most High's angels by damaging the baby's soul which is the seat of her emotions", whispered Rakeem. "Tell me more," mumbled Darfur. Since her body has trillions of cells, we caused her glands to malfunction, producing hormone imbalances across the electrical grid of her body that's controlled by our disembodied voices who are ruling her mind right now as we speak". Darfur laughed and said, "Inexplicable," while whirling his whip like tail playfully behind his massive wings, with a glowing rattler on its tip. "I saw the pastor in the admission room being interviewed by the perspicacious counselor where they were asking him about his daughter's medical history, with many questions ranging from diabetes, hypertension, and mental disease. He answered yes to all the family mental history questions which are substantiating evidence we have permission to channel her mind with our demonic voices". "How wonderful," whispered Darfur. "Before they give her anti-psychotic meds, the mind controlling pills, Demon-Freeze will be performing dark whispering in her ears with a frequency of debilitative soundwaves that will trigger her brain to lose conscious of reality. She really talks to her conscious out loud." With excitement in his raspy voice, Darfur squealed in darkness and screamed with an ecstasy beyond a reality like someone who won a billion dollar lottery. Then he said, "When she finish that assignment, I am sending her to work with Zia, our mistress of the dead, who has the gift to talk to the living and the dead of the netherworld. She is mind bending at the bewitching hours from 12am to 3am to experiment with the new Teleportation gift I imparted to her that defies the laws of physics, by shifting her through the atoms like one of our demons activating three-dimensional airwave manipulation. Now you see me, and now you don't, is the gift that will intrigue her for some years to come. She has sent us many dark petitions to curse this Sid. I am aiming to please her once and for all".

There were powerful, mysterious consecrated prayers Sid had prayed over Ishkooda, requesting warrior angels to block and dismantle witchcraft trafficking by deploying the warrior angels to the north, east, south, and west. But Darfur persisted with his proliferation of evil treasures to aggrandize Zia's dynasty in the earth realm. Sid was trying desperately to secure visitation privileges to visit the psyche ward and liberate the pastor's daughter with his powerful prayers taught to him by the Most High. But the Psychiatric ward visitation policies were influenced by the regional devilish Principalities which motivated the doctor's board of trustees to draft a body of laws restricting patient visits only to relatives. Sid was not to be outdone; he stood in the gap for her interceding and fasting until they eventually gave her weekend passes to visit her home.

Wounds of a Fallen Angel

"I adore you most Holy One," whispered Sid to the Most High after long hours of prayer in his secret chambers located down in his basement. The basement is where he and his Jack Russell dog name "Coco" spent most of their time lounging. After spiritual warfare, he looked up and saw a fracture of moonstone-yellow bright lights peeping through the Ecclesiastic jet black sky. Apparitions of dark ebony lights transverse between the towering trees in a menacing way around his home. Grisly spores that were sprinkling the ground with toxic gremlin dust had covered his lawn around his property. Sid gift of discerning of spirits was in full operation, so his reasoning and intellect was bypass and superseded by the Spirit of Liberty. He saw in the Spirit, a muscular thick thigh creature with stiletto shaped long venomous fingernails, and vine like green blood vessels, squirming under his fleshy membranes, creeping syrup slow motion under the sprawling boughs of the antediluvian ancient sycamore tree in his courtyard. Sid was witnessing a stalking cosmic creature better known as a fallen angel that was wounded most likely by a warrior angel from the Most High. He gathered this was probably from the spiritual warfare days ago when he was under attack by the unseen empire of darkness. The wounded creature was prowling under the moss-infested tree with balletic grace and lion-like power. He was staring with two bleak eyes in eerie foreboding, with a defined cheekbone over a square and firm marble jaw that was chiseled by the hands of the Creator. It was almost enthralling to look upon his swirling Scandinavian dark hair that danced in the dark gothic wind. His trance-like glaring eyes were bloodshot and gleaming with anger each passing minute. This fiendish beast was in excruciating mental pain, and looking for revenge, as he sucked air through his fangs like a cobra, to detect angel DNA in the vicinity. As he gripped the branches with his cold sweaty hands, and herculean supernatural strength, you could see spiky bones and open wounds beneath his ossified membranes on his celestial wings. Below the skirt of the tree, melting oozing lubricated intestines had spilled out, and splashed on the naked ground.

Green bubbling pulsating entrails from his bowels was seeping into the ground below that gave off a putrefying stench of a thousand rottening corpses. These angels were immortal with a recovery anointing that automatically healed and restored any of their wounds within Kairos minutes. Some of the angel DNA also squirted in a close nearby pond filled with minnows. The small one-inch minnows grew four feet long with meat eating white serrated teeth because of the angel fluid contaminating the pond. As they splashed and slapped the pond dry, the hybrid-minnows began to devour each other, like savage red belly hungry piranhas. They gnawed, and masticated each other to death, as the crunching of fish bones resonated in the longitudinal flowing airwaves. Suddenly, Sid spirituals eyes were disconnected, he could no longer see the wounded gelid eye devil, even though he tried desperately with his natural baby blue eyes. The gift of discerning of spirits had shut down his insight into the spiritual realm, like a DVR movie place on pause. The gift of discerning of spirits was a divine ability given to Sid from the Third Heaven that gave him insight into the multi-dimensional spiritual realm, where angels and demons were visible to his spiritual eyes when the gift manifested. For this episode, the gift was in operation for only seven seconds. "Oh no," shouted Sid! "LORD, please let me witness the final phase of this battle." Sid, whispering shallowly from his lungs, remembered when he was decreeing earlier, there was a bombardment of arrows from the third heaven, showering the second heaven airways, with lightning like speed targeting sphinx headed dark angels, where piercing screeches escape their paltry mouths in a fit of rage. He realized that he was spiritually positioned in heavenly places with the Most High even though he was physcally still in the flesh. So when he shouted fire as a commanding chief in the military, there was a blizzard of flaming arrows whizzing, and whistling through the sky chasing evil angels, into hidden decommission. This action altered the northeastern wind currents, and the acoustic soundwaves, generating magnetic storms hijacking the airways for the Most High. The hidden watchers were assigned to protect him, without Sid being aware of their presence. Sid knew divine reinforcement and intervention came to his assistance in the battle, to put down satanic resistance. He was wondering why this mysterious attack was launched against him. Their attack was unsuccessful against him because he was still protected by the Third Heaven Divine Angelic Assistance Team. These rebellious sphinx headed devils hadn't received permission from the 3rd heaven for clearance to attack.

Flea Market Idols

His basement window was left slightly open from last night, to allow some cool air to flow in, which he later forgot to close. Then suddenly a pair of halogen-blue eyes begin to glow and illuminate like glittering diamond dust against the jet black nightfall, staring right at Sid through the window, while condensation trickled down the window panes like dripping demon saliva. It was one of the demonic foot soldiers, Demon-Freeze, from the kingdom of darkness that was assigned to him by one of his adversaries; the witches palm reading fortuneteller's society. An ex-girlfriend of his became bitter and vindictive toward him when he called the relationship off because she wanted him to have dark communion by drinking a small cup of human blood she stole from a hospital laboratory when she was being treated for strep throat due from kissing dead bodies in a funeral home. The oily looking blood had a salty, fishy taste to it when she took a sip that eventually made her nauseated.

She had a tridimensional relationship with the palm reading fortunetellers by practicing witchcraft secretly that tied their soul, spirit, and body together with a bond that drove Sid further away which eventually starved their relationship, bringing it to a slow death. She pretended to be a loving Christian in his presence, but her worship of the earth, water, fire, and air was her main attraction. Her name was Zia. She tried to put a curse on Sid after they broke up, but each time the curse would swiftly return with an incomplete mission status. Something was blocking the curse. With the help of Darfur, Zia had programmed curses in the Sun, Moon, and Stars against him but they never worked. Sid was a praying man that walked upright before the Most High who created the heavens. His relatives originally migrated from Europe, but through divine intervention, he ended up in Ishkooda.

Now the entity at the window was one of the shapeshifter angels that fell from the second heaven while trying to deflect Sid prayers from reaching the third heaven, where the Supreme King of Glory resides. With fear causing Sid knees to wobble, and tremble, the shapeshifting spirit transformed into an image of a wet slithery black mamba snake which could detect heat through its infrared design built-in sensory system. Coco, Sid's dog, started growling and barking with his right front leg pointing at the window. Sid kept right on praying while opening one eye with the other one shut, trying to keep an eye on Coco because he could sense he was on to something in the room. His late grandma had always told him that animals like dogs are sensitive to the spiritual world, especially the treading serpentine demons. When demons were casted out of candidates in her home ministry, her pet house dogs would scatter, and run with abandonment all over the house. They reacted that way because once the elusive demons were casted out, they would chase the dogs to inhabit their bodies. It was illegal for demons to walk the earth without bodies.

She was a great prayer warrior that spent her entire life in Deliverance Ministry casting out devils and combating spiritual warfare against the Kingdom of darkness. It was said when she was dying, they heard her saying at her last breath,

"Satan get thee behind me, in the name of the Most High,"
then she gave up the ghost.

In undulating locomotion, the demonic black mamba
propelled forward slowly sliding under Sid's bed for refuge.
Then suddenly the serpent saw a miniature Babylonian
sundial sitting on the floor. She immediately teleported right
into it hiding. It was a cursed item that Sid brought into his
house unknowingly from a flea market sale about three miles
south from the outskirts of Ishkooda. The sundial had
hieroglyphics on its surface with an encoded message. The
decrypted message translated meant "Worship the Prince of
Darkness divine protector of Earth," which Sid never knew.
Horus according to the ancient eastern religion was the
Invincible Sky god whose left eye was the moon, and his right
eye was the sun. However, Sid never knew how to interpret
hieroglyphics, so that is why he loved buying pictorial art. If he
knew the item represented a pagan god other than the Most
High he would have burned it to ashes and repented.

The demon was in suspense about Sid detection of her presence, so she began to summon assistance through her psychic mind powers for backup since the cursed item gave her legal access to Sid's home.

There was a known practice of the Ishkoodians to donate their decease relative's clothes to the busy Mega Flea market to help those in need so that a charity deduction could be applied toward their taxes the next following year. You could find all kinds of second hand zoot suits, ball dresses, snakeskin shoes, tuxedo hats, pleated skirts, designer blue jeans, wool coats, leopard jackets, and many other garments on sale at the flea market at an unbelievable cheat price. People from all three working classes in the little town would line up at the store doors early in the morning hoping to be the first to jump on the best bargains as people do on Black Fridays during the major holidays. A year ago, two women hungry for a hot bargain, got into a violent hair pulling fight over a pair of battery operated flashing rhinestone cowboy pink jeans in the middle of the store that was priced one dollar.

But what they didn't know, the jeans were once worn by a deranged serial killer that received the death penalty by lethal injection. Each irritated woman gasping for breath, grabbed a leg of the pants clenched fist tight, pulling and jerking it in the opposite direction, like a contested tug of war, trying to snatch the jeans from each other. Eventually, the cops were immediately called to put down the fisticuff. After they interrogated both parties, they gave the jeans to a tall tobacco chewing, diva nose, blond headed female with Venus-red fingernails. Two weeks later, the same lady who paid a dollar for the jeans, was arrested for murdering her sister-in-law with an aluminum baseball bat at a rental center when they got into a heated argument over a parking space. The arresting officer who was trained to pay attention to detail, noticed she was wearing the same battery operating rhinestone cowboy jeans at the crime scene he released to her at the flea market. As she sat in the detention center waiting to be processed for murder, she kept saying to an obese officer, "The voices told me to kill her," while the rhinestone flashing jeans begin to wane as the batteries got weak. There was a dark hidden secret about the history of the pink cowboy jeans that belong to the serial killer. It was documented that the female serial killer who murdered little babies in odd numbered months, was demon possessed by Shanghai demons released from triple dark satanic graveyards. Back then, the church community lived in fear because the serial killer sent group text messages on cheap throw away cell phones to pregnant church member's smartphones warning them that their babies must be sacrifice. The serial killer would dress up like a missionary to infiltrate the local churches and synagogues to collect intelligence from the prophets when they spoke advance knowledge prophetically to the expecting mothers about their unborn babies' future. When the prophet prophesied to a mother that her baby would be a great evangelist or church leader, the serial killer would take a snapshot of the woman, and make plans to destroy her seed to block them from leading multitudes to the Most High in the future. There were many attempts by the local priesthood to cast the devils out of the woman, but the fiendish diabolical beast refused to relinquish his control over her, because of mysterious legal rights. Because they spiritually misdiagnose the type of demons possessing her, they were drained of their energy and strength trying to cast them out. The mystery behind their demise was the Shanghai vampire demons who do not drain you of your blood but they drain you of your physical energy to make you quit the exorcism by giving in to discouragement, mental burnout, ineffectiveness, and wrong diagnoses. When she stared at one of the trembling high priests with her ferocious smaragdine hypnotic eyes, he begin to lose control of his bladder, as she spoke allegiance to Satan with a stentorian volcanic voice speaking in tongues backwards.

Her execution was botched because the warden had to order six times the normal dosage of pentobarbital for the injection, after hours of out-bursting laughter from the killer with swirling black-wood smoke emerging from her mouth in the shape of misty coiling serpents. During the first two attempts the woman snapped the restraining belts like breaking a piece of thread, then with demonic supernatural strength she fought twenty scrambling security guards running like they were under the influence of prune juice before she succumbed to the drug. After her death, the strongman demon with many other lower class devils decided to transfer from her lifeless body by soundwaves right into her pink rhinestone cowboy jeans, like energy stored in alkaline batteries. They preferred a body, but a decision was made by the demons to transfer into the jeans as a temporary holding station until the next person wore the pink jeans so they could transfer or attach to their body. So when the jeans arrived at the flea market years ago, that's when the demons saw their opportunity to transfer to the blond headed woman who made the purchase.

Whenever Sid purchased his clothes, he would always pray over them before bringing them home, whether they were new or used. One day he witnessed devil worshippers trying on pants in a department store changing room, they intentionally left voodoo chicken feet in the new pants pockets they decided not to buy, placing the pants back on the store rack for the next innocent shopper to buy. He covered all areas of his life with prayer, but the purchased idol he bought from the

flea market stirred up the secret abyss and dark secret agents

of the evil empire.

Warning: Viewer Discretion Advised

Suddenly, the dark shadows descended without warning after an awful massive period of silence expired in the first heaven. An apparition appeared glowing inwardly with a purple flashing flame in its transparent belly releasing hot molecular gases from its stinger saturating the atmosphere with radioactive dark energy. Hell was about to host a new visitor. A blare in the immortal realms of dire black lights, strange shadow-wing creatures, prowled silently in dark nightshade, waiting for the next lost soul. Was it too late to pray? Ebola pregnant demons with ebony ivory horns, dragging lifeless souls into black gaping cesspool pits that writhe and coiled with glee. A labyrinth of insidious seeping mist was loitering in the foul-smelling fecal air as creatures bathe and swim joyfully in cesspools full of excrements stirring up bubble baths. Bursting bubbles release a stench that could even make cadavers cover their noses. The dark oracles of death, breathe enchanting whispers, unlocking the underground forbidden gates, opening doorway portals to the black Abyss. As Hades was lathering himself up in a foaming rage of vomit, death kneeled down in unfathomable agony. Deadly shrieks of wailing pierced the decaying air in realms of darkness. Then a hush escaped the bosom of Hell, as a mysterious silence drifted into infinity. In the midst of the Abyss, was the stalking curve fur back beast with dreadful energy and hungry eyes, inhaling voodoo vapor through his deep nostrils while gurgling and guzzling on human remains. Suddenly a thump at the gates of the Abyss, startled him as the metal doors swung open. A loud shriek pierced the darkness, energized with chaotic energy. There descending from the sky was a ferocious infernal beast with yellow glowing eyes, speeding quickly toward the open giant metal gates, with a screaming, terrified little boy clenched tightly snugged in his massive hairy arms in flight, as two Holy Angels gave chase in hot pursuit, on his trail through the nebulous Jetstream. After the angels closed the gap of distance between each other with blinding speed, one of the angels grabbed the slimy thick tail of the elusive creature right before he barely escaped into the entrance of the black portal. The squealing beast quickly spun around with terror in his bloodshot eyes, swinging savagely with vicious death blows at the powerful angels. The evasive angel ripped the beast's slimy tail from his body that magically morphed into a massive viper coiling himself quickly around the Warrior Angel's body. The serpent wrestling angel, yelled out to his partner, "Quickly, pursue and rescue the child, for his sister prayers we were dispatch to protect him," cried the Angel as he gripped and crushed the snapping serpent's mouth with his powerful hands.

A trail of luminol vapor swirled in the sky like coronary arteries that led the destiny Angel within seconds of the wounded beast. Squeezing the little boy tightly with a strong grip, he was hiding in a thunder cloud under 666 sheets of hidden lights within the four layers of the atmosphere, teleporting to the third dimension. The Angel scanning the skies and earth, with his infrared night vision, detected demon DNA and quickly unsheathed his sword. He was within 70 feet of the beast as he soared gliding closer sniffing the air, as the stench of the beast revealed his hideout. The Angel translated and teleported into the dimension he was hiding in, and there they were, face to face, exchanging angry ferocious glares with unblinking eyes. The growling beast said, "I can already taste your blood." Too close to swing their swords, they grabbed each other's wrist and tussled in the sky like two giant Angelic Gladiators battling in the unseen dimension. Thunder rumbled, and lightning flashed as the battle escalated. After trading insults, they stepped back swinging as their two swords clanged against each other, then the awkward beast charged forward to thrust him with the sharp blade, but the side stepping graceful Angel jumped on a passing cloud and with a flicked of his wrist he flipped his somersaulting sword at the beast's legs barely missing him as the beast back flipped in the air and landed flat footed on the snarling cloud, sniggling saying, "Too slow boy". The somersaulting sword boomerang back to the Angel's hand and both charged each other again, crossing their swords, locking them together, they were face to face again. Miraculously the little boy wriggled himself loose from the beast grip and jumped on the angels back holding his wings tightly. When the Beast took his eyes off the Angel looking for the boy, the Angel quickly spun around in a 360 degree circle and delivered a slicing blow to his head, decapitating the Beast. Sid quickly sat up in his bed sweating and gasping for air. This angelic battle was only a dream.

Down in the depths of the earth, Canyon, the gatekeeper of the subterranean territorial region that covered Ishkooda, received an encrypted frequency from Darfur headquarters from the second heaven authorizing the release of creeping spirits from the Southgate forest adjacent from Sid's house. These were the darting speed merchant demons that seem to always escape human eyes by running like a blur. They were preparing to surround his home to replace any demonic foot soldier that was cast out by Sid when Demon-Freeze, the stronghold shapeshifting demon, made her move. Canyon smiled with a lopsided grin. As his smile expanded, you could see the bleach white alpha canine teeth protruding from his mouth scarred with blood stains and dripping with saliva from a voracious evil appetite. He sent a message to the imps right below the foundation of Sid's house better known as the underground gate. He was ordering them to be ready to open the gate at his command in the pitch blackness. No demon will be allowed through the gate unless he says Belial-Baphomet. This is the evil empires linguistic password for passage when the battle begins in Ishkooda.

Witch Secrets

"I wonder why the curse we chanted over Sid's picture has never taken place." This was Zia speaking to one of her witch friends in the palm reading fortune teller's society where she's a member. The night had finally dissolved into the morning dimming lights where there was a haunting beauty hovering above the high rising apartments where she spent her bewitching hours. Silky soaring sweeps of air blowing from her cheap desktop fan caused her hair to break dance with intensity while she pondered over vengeance toward Sid. "How do you know it hasn't taken place," said her friend? "Because I drove past his house the other day and he was standing outside watering his stinky flowers." "Did you stand in the middle of the pentagram when you chanted the curse," said her friend? "Yes, I did"! "Did you burn his picture after you put a curse on it with demonic incantations as well"? "For the last time, yes I did! What's that foul smell I keep getting a whiff of every now and then", said Zia? "It's the tuna sandwich that's been sitting on the kitchen table since last week that I bought."

"Don't you think it's time to dispose of it Miss know it all"?

"Yeah, it figures, you're just upset that the curse enforced by the shadow of darkness isn't working on Sid." "Oh yeah," sarcastically shouts Zia! "I'll sell my soul to the Satan before I let him get away from dissing me. No one has ever turned me down and live to tell about it".

Two weeks ago Zia, the mistress of the dead, burned pumpkin spice scented black candles that flickered with fork like flames as wall shadows danced seductively with coils of serpent like smoke drifting over her haunting altar worshipping the dead.

Her intimacy with the Kingdom of Darkness was a contractual adulterous love affair passed down from her banshee red bloodline from thirteen ancestry generations. All of her late auntie's were aggressive witches, but strangely their lives ended prematurely, after dueling powerful prophetical men in spiritual warfare.

With silky kohl black eyelashes highlighting her irresistible dreamy emerald doll eyes, Zia attractiveness lured many godly men into her satanic snare.

One flash of her halo white teeth gleaming from her glamour shot face, set them up for a hypnotized rendezvous with her voluptuous hour glass figure. Her motive was to date anointed Christian men, so she could wage war against the Most High by slaying them spiritually, therefore weakening the ranks in his glorious church.

The sloping Bermuda lawn in the backyard was parsley lush green while crooning pigeons were busy plucking up wrinkle spoiled fruit that fell from the towering fertile fig tree. A former yardman had overcharged her for grass fertilizer, and she put a curse on his yard, where grass has not grown for six years. There was a secret hidden in the lacquer clear lake behind her home, where spotted bream fish flip flopped and bombed dive into the mystical, enchanting body of water. The crypt still rippling lake was reservoir round, and shimmering, as an army of horse flies drone over its fathomless bottom. It was hemmed in by precipitous hills with lines of pine trees where the hollowness of the valley magnified all sounds. The wind exhaled, and breathe through the gnarly bushes, as the twisting trees started stripping their rustling leaves, succumbing to sensual naked sorcery.

There were five corked bottles resting on the bottom of the mirror lake bed with twenty pound cylinder cement blocks tied to each one that had a scroll inside. For every woman or man that offended her, would end up inside the corked cursed bottle with their name listed on the scroll. At her evil picture altar, she would pin pictures around her altar that she stole from her enemies. She would also work the late shift on her job with the federal government because she had secret motives. When her co-workers clocked out for the day, at night she would ride the elevator to sneak around the eleven floors to steal pictures off their desk, or leftover bottle water that had their DNA on it as a substitute. Some would ignorantly give pictures to her when she ask, not knowing that hell was setting them up for a dark surprise. She also hacked computer social media accounts and stole images from webpages to use in her wicked séances. Next, she would deploy evil spirits to go on a seek and destroy mission for the ones that are on the pictures showing no mercy. If she inject the photograph with satanic needles, then demons would afflict the person with sickness and diseases. Then Zia would run to her voodoo altar and sculpture an image with carving wood that represented those on the picture. Without hesitation, she would choke, cut, beat, and spit on the wooden doll afflicting and tormenting her enemies in the physical realms. Also stolen strands of hair from combs and hair brushes of co-workers were burned to release spells upon lukewarm disobedient believers. Those that were not protected under the Blood of the Most High's Son would end up in the care of a physician with an unexplainable diagnosis.

Finally, she would scribble all of her enemies' names on a sheet of paper for the marine spirit curse. Then she would begin incantations saying, "Death to your careers, you will never be promoted while your life will be a platform to launch everybody else career to the next level for increases. Death to your finances, you will never get ahead, and those that are behind you will always prosper while you stay in debt. Death to your health, you will never be healed but medicated for the rest of your life." Finally she would invoke the names of her gods after rolling the paper up into an evil scroll before sealing it. The scroll would be placed in a bottle then corked. Next, a twenty pound cement block was tied to the bottle with stolen dental floss strings from her local dentist garbage dumpster. Before dropping it into the lake, she would say, "As long as this bottle is under this lake so shall this curse be enforced by the mighty marine spirit. As long as this bottle is on the bottom of the lake, so shall all of their careers, salaries, and health. So, therefore, it is seal and enforced by the gods of the Pharaohs." Then the cadaverous sky gave birth to a ghostly grey Baphomet shape cloud with a humming sound of legions of winged demons sounding like low speed hair dryers on assignment to enforce the curse. Bad things happened to everyone on her list but one person. She could not curse Sid.

He prayed spiritual warfare decrees counter-attacking the
forces of darkness daily.

After the Storm

"Whew! I didn't get much sleep last night", said Sid lying in his silky smooth Cortinella French style bed, stretching his arms over his head trying to wake up with his eyes tightly shut. Each night he prayed divine protection over himself as he slept defenseless melting under his Persian satin smooth sheets. In the adjacent room, his invisible guardian angel dressed in an ankle length white cassock robe with a golden sash was standing in the doorway with folded arms and massive shoulders beneath his wings watching over him with high voltage glowing laser beam eyes to deter evil while he slept. The next morning with the glowing honey mustard sun splashing through his tantalizing tinted bay windows, he remembered surviving a nightmare dream where he escaped a pit full of coiling hungry Burmese pythons when he started singing a hymn.

Suddenly his ringing and vibrating cellphone lying next to his bed on his marble top night stand started playing a ringtone called, "There is a fountain filled with Blood," that alerted him to answer the phone quickly. He kicked his way out of his satin sheets with his long legs like he was kickboxing ghosts and hurriedly reached over to the night stand grabbing the loud musical cellphone. Before grabbing the phone he knew that it was his sister because he had programmed the phone to play a spiritual ringtone when she call so that he could assist her in the Deliverance Ministry. She never called him to gossip, but it was always strictly business to help someone that needed assistance with salvation.

He said, "Hello, what's up Sheila, while sitting on the side of his bed?" All he could hear was a child constantly screaming to the top of her lungs, and whining perpetually while Sid's sister was hollering in the background for Sid to pray, and assist her in the child's deliverance. She took the phone off the amplifier speaker, and started speaking in a rushing tone to Sid saying, "This child has been screaming and crying for about three hours nonstop." Sid said, "Have you changed her pamper"? Sheila said, "Yes." "Have you fed her" he shouted? She said, "Yes"! "Have you heard her burp or belch," he said trying to shout over the crying baby's voice? "Yes to all your questions," Sheila cried. "Her mother is here who just picked her up from the doctor's office, and he couldn't do nothing about the problem but prescribe teething medicine. Oh, by the way, she is not teething neither." "I have one more question for you," he said in a resigning voice. "Does her mother smoke pot or do crack," he whispered under his voice? Then Sheila said, "She's the pastor's wife, Sid." Then the phone went silent for about ten seconds. Sid thought he had lost connection, so he looked at the phone screen, and saw it still was connected. Then immediately the Most High spoke to him, interpreting his dream he had the night before, about deliverance from the pythons when he started singing a hymn. The Most High said, "In the dream the pythons are devils, and your anointed music ministry is the hymn that will deliver the baby." Sid knew right away that music would deliver the baby from the crying spell base on the revelation he just received. "The demons are tormenting the baby who were symbolically the pythons in the dream I had" he spoke to himself. "Can babies see demons," he whispered? Then coincidentally the phone reconnected with Sheila screaming, "Hellooooooooo, hello, are you there Sid"?

Sid said, "Sheila I am here, and I have the healing answer for the baby." "Oh praise the Lord for he is worthy to be praise," she said with exhilaration as the baby continued to cry.

He said, "Activate your speaker amplifier on your cellphone, and put it in the baby's bassinet close to her, so she can hear the sound coming from its speaker." "Okay, I have completed the assignment Sid," she said while waiting patiently for deliverance.

Sid activated his speaker on his cellphone and placed it on his night stand, then he dropped to his knees to grab his soprano saxophone from under his bed, so he could prepare to play an anointed solo through the phone to drive the unfathomable demons away from the baby. He started blowing his anointed breath through the instrument, playing the song Amazing Grace through the cell phone speaker that started shifting the atmosphere releasing the Shekinah glory which was the presence of the Most High around the baby. Suddenly the baby uncontrollable screaming and whining stop. Then she started coughing and gasping for air for a few seconds, then her breathing return to normal again. Sheila and the baby's mother stared at each other marveling over the change in the child's behavior. When Sid finish playing his last scale by descending softly ending the song, he notice a mausoleum like silence on the phone speaker. Then Sheila said, "The baby is healed and smiling." Sid raised his hands over his head glorifying the Most High but his invisible guardian angel quickly grabbed his sword from his sheath, walking in slow motion toward the cellphone stepping with one foot in front of the other, ready to fight because he detected unclean spirits trying to channel themselves behind the scene through the phone like uninvited bullet ants. When the misty unclean spirits arrived through Sid's phone radio frequency and saw the Angel with his two thousand degree flaming hot sword, they quickly dived back into Sid's speaker on his cellphone, returning back through the telecommunications frequency over the towers back to Sheila's place. Sid unaware of the unclean spirits tactics, walked over to his phone to pick it up when suddenly there was an ear piercing scream that startled him. He said, "What's wrong," as his heartbeat race in his chest while fumbling his phone? The pastor's wife started trembling and stuttering pointing up at the window above the baby saying, "Look"! There squatting on the window sill was a simian eyed inflated head demon, with slimy maggot infected oleaginous black hair. He also had eight leech like blood sucking tentacles with open pus oozing sores wriggling from his belly. The creature was scratching his broom bushy rabid tail raw where thousands of crawling fleas were fighting bulging ticks for a dry patch of skin. When he lick out his raspy psychedelic tongue like a dragon lizard, a cloud of flying scorpion tail biting flies ascended from his mouth that could spray flesh melting poison from its lips into the eyes of its prey bringing instant blindness.

The glowing yellow eyed demon with a quadruple row of wrinkled forehead skin, was grinning with his wicked jaws, showing all of his drooling fin shape incisors to the ladies and puckering his juicy gaping lips while fire and smoke escaped from his nostrils. Sheila shaking uncontrollably, started walking backwards slowly, crying out from her belly with a loud voice saying, "Be gone demon and never return to this child again, in the name of Yeshua"! The squealing demon screamed as if he was on fire, dropping a baby's pacifier and vanished in the thin air leaving a putrid smell behind.

Eyes have not seen

Up in the Third heaven, there was divine judgement flowing as smooth as syrup, down the north latitude like a sapphire blue waterfall parallel down to the earthly town of Ishkooda according to the heavenly orbit calculations. Righteousness and holiness were streaming into a pool of light echoes that rippled with undulating sound waves of love flickering like sparkling glitter on its surface. The fragrance of heaven was emanating with acoustic oscillation from the glassy swirling pools. It was so much light illuminating the expansion of the firmament that the naked human eye would suffer a Bartimaeus blindness after looking upon it. The creativity and craftsmanship up there were as flawless as the heart of a divine diamond, more than nine hundred trillion light years away. There were counter-circulating streams of mercy encircling a sparkling and dazzling censer full of smoke with voices that could be heard like shallow echoes in deep valleys summoning divine assistance. The voices in the glowing censer were the prayers of many souls that cried out to the

Most High down in the earth realm. Most of the prayers carried by secret messenger angels that reach the throne room were attacked unsuccessfully by the Kingdom of Darkness. They traveled at a speed of 186,000 miles per second while leaving an electromagnetic spectrum streaking trail of illumination behind their divine wings that could not be detected by the human eye. The anti-prayer gargoyle angels with fluorescent tinted eyes patrolled the voodoo airspace that these spiritual prayers covertly had to travel through to reach their destination. Giant Neutron stars in the heavens were programmed by cannibalistic subway devils underground in the earth realm to electromagnetically emit beams of lights that pulsated secret radio waves alerting the Principalities when prayers were preparing to enter the voodoo airspace. This is one of the orbiting systems that triggered these warriors when the prayers began to travel through the first and second heavens. Most of them carried an anointing that was hotter than Hell's fire which causes these goblins to scream, and beg for death even though they were immortal. Some prayers were attacked mercilessly like a swarm of African killer bees causing the secret messenger angels to release a bowel loosening scream which radioed for backup assistance. Traveling 650 million miles per hour, backup sparkling silver fire winged Seraphim angels would liberate the stunned messenger angel, but the prayer would temporarily be hindered by the evil empire because of the rules of engagement. This delayed process caused some believers to doubt their prayers in the earth realm. Snatching and grabbing prayers in the second heaven were similar to purse snatching in the earth realm originated by Satan, the world's notorious thief. The devils were programmed to attack these prayers violently like a pack of bloodthirsty flying raptors. These flying celestial moon-shadow archangels were built like F-16 jets in the no-prayer fly zone under the jurisdiction of the second heaven. Once they identified a godly prayer traveling through the no fly-zone protected by the anti-prayer Lucifer defense system, the Ruler of Darkness would assign anti-prayer entities to stop these messages from reaching their destination. When the atmosphere appeared to be tranquil and peaceful with serene energy, then it immediately shifted to a ruthless battleground with deadly assaults occurring throughout the day. Then a mystery was revealed. Sometimes the angels would yield to some secret messengers with prayers and allow them to travel through the no fly zone when the gamma rays started bursting. This sign indicated that the demonic foot soldiers in the earth realm had influenced the believer to petition the Most High for something against his Divine will and purpose. These are the prayers some Ishkoodians would say, be careful what you ask for because you just may get it. When prayers were postmarked spiritually as next day delivery, powerful Seraphim Angels would transfer the prayers. They were arm and extremely dangerous.

The Most High secret messengers are his speed delivery angels that are on assignment for transferring prayers for his people from the first heaven through the second heaven to the third heaven. These angels had to travel as fast as light through many dangerous galaxies in the second heaven voodoo air space where rebellious giant angels are better known as Principalities ruled over certain geographical areas and airways. Getting pass the second heaven was always a challenge for the divine angels before they could reach the 3rd heaven border. Anytime an answer was sent in return by the Most High to these prayers then a battle of a more formidable opponent from the evil empire was assigned to block it. When you hear colossal stars exploding sending shockwaves through the clouds of gas, then the bad boys showed up on the scene called the Princes.

So many in Sid's neighborhood did not realize every spoken word that proceeded out of their mouths were assigned to either an angel or demon to bring them either a blessing or cursing. Negative confessions by people were monitored and recorded by the Kingdom of Satan to reward them with a curse that most humans were unaware. They would confiscate the word frequencies in secretly hidden studio containers so they can be used as evidence against the believers when they were ready to be exposed by the Satanic Confession Militia Task Force. Godly word confessions were recorded by the Third Heaven godly angels to bring blessings.

These acoustic words were pregnant with an explosive anointing that was too hot for the devils to handle. Satanic angels would receive first degree holy burns if they got too close to some of the declaration frequencies. There were blessings and curses but nothing between the two. Sid knew death and life was in the power of his tongue, so he always put a watch before his mouth. Every morning before sunrise, he would perform positive word confessions derive from the sixty six books he studied daily. He knew evils words that were spoken today would come back and haunt him tomorrow even after he forgot what he said. Demons were on high alert whenever he spoke. A code blue would be announced by the demonic world whenever he started casting out evil spirits. His mouth was weaponized because of the scriptures he meditated on night and day. Demons would say secretly, "His lips was like a machine gun because he always hit moving targets with his words." They were referring to themselves as the moving targets. For every weapon of destruction sent to him by the kingdom of darkness, he would command it to backfire and return to sender with double disgrace and triple shame. Then the dark clouds were arrested and banished by the eternal Third Heaven fire release by his prayer.

Heavenly Court

As time passed, there was a spiritual meeting that was commencing in the Throne Room high above in the 3rd Heaven where the stars converge into bright heavenly constellations, and numerous galaxies far away. The stars with infrared lights in Orion and Mazzaroth were sparkling like angel-fire reflecting off the succubus-black dark energy. Something began to twinkle and dazzle like beautiful waves of submerging lights in its midst. Suddenly, there appeared two tall escort angels that were powerful and wonderful to look upon with twisted veins of lightning flashing from their wings when they flapped them in flight. An aura of electromagnetic energies of infrared radiation and atomic hydrogen surrounded their glistering bodies when they maneuvered around incoming meteorites. These rarely seen angels had glowing emerald green Saturn shaped eyes that flickered like a passion of fire. This class of electrifying angels also displayed a deadly celestial stare that penetrated and pierced to the core of one's soul when they were escorting in the airwaves with purpose and authority. They were escorting subpoenaed representatives from the Kingdom of Darkness to testify as witnesses before the assembly of counselors clothed in armors of light appointed over a case called Sid vs. the Kingdom of Darkness. The Bailiff Angel moving with leopard-like grace cried foghorn loud, "Please be seated"! "Oh no, not yet," said a fiery Seraphim with six wings and star flame gold hair! With bedazzling genesis-green eyes that were the gateway to his soul, he began to appeal to the visitors in a deep bass vibrating voice. "We can't commence now because some other dark angels from the second heaven have not arrived yet." Then one of the representatives from the Kingdom of Darkness that looked like he had been dipped in a pool of shiny black oil, whispered to another fellow demon close by. "He's the one that clashed with the North Westside Kingdom of Darkness about a year ago." "Who won the fight, said the other demon"? "Well, the North Westside Archangel had to summon the assistance of the South-side Prince of Birmingham because that six wing juggernaut glowed inwardly with white lights that burned and blinded anything within a one-mile radius in the second heaven. Then after doing that he transformed himself into an invisible vortex of destructible blazing heat, releasing a nebula of wavy radiation that blasted, and scorched all the wicked east-side and west-side paramilitary forces." After the heavenly battle, there was a trail of celestial hot plasma flesh from those forces that glowed like green hot stones in the galaxy. Of course, they can regenerate their angelic flesh like the chameleon lizards do when they lose their tails which caused them to shed the old locust armor for a new suit after they warred with that Seraphim. "Shhh! He's coming our way", said the demon storyteller in a quiet tone. Then the Seraphim ascended with a stroking motion of flapping up and down with his rainbow-like Neotropical wings beating the air. He landed like a descending drone, face to face with the Kingdom of Darkness representatives with the Escort Angels standing close by. "Where's your legal litigation team," said the silver fire wing Seraphim speaking in an authoritative voice to the demons? "Ugh, Ugh! They should be here in a moment," whispered a demon in multiple voice tones because he has the ability to change his voice and imitate any sound like a ventriloquist. "Well if they are not here when the mighty Cherubim stands in the secret place of the Most High presence for the roll call in this court case then one of you all will have to adopt this case or drop the charges against Sid." One evil angel in the entourage who was known for a sudden outburst of rage and verbal abuse was warned by the storyteller demon to refrain from saying any blasphemous word in the courtroom because he would be banned to the black abyss with no mercy by the presiding Judge. His cohorts noticed that he became perturbed and irritated when the Seraphim gave his ultimatum.

Permission to Attack

As scenes switched from the heavens to the earth realm, a Street preaching missionary could be heard in a whispery raspy, hoarse voice crying out in a staccato cadence tone saying, "The babies, the babies can see fallen angels," while holding her Gucci handbag tucked under her left arm. Her face glowed like the setting sun while she held a wireless VHF microphone right against her chapped, dry silicone enhanced lips preaching in her champagne fake snake skin high heel shoes. She always fasted five times a week which transcended and elevated her vision to see the supernatural world like prophets. Suddenly she had an open vision seeing a battalion of muscular black headed dragonfly like angels with blue steel radiator coils protruding from under their sheet plated barrel chest flying toward a gated community. These cadaverous nose demonic angels spitted like cobra's every fifty miles when they locked their wings gliding so they could mark the airways just in case they needed backup tracking assistance as they soared in the eastern winds.

The morning buzz circulating among holy angels in the throne room was that Sid's case might be on shaky ground because of that cursed item he purchased from the Mega Flea Market. The kingdom of darkness was seeking permission from the Most High to attack him for a violation of his holy commandments. He bought the Babylonian sundial from a feeble elderly lady that had a booth there for the last ten years. Sid didn't know that the little old humpback lady was a disciple of the Satanic Worship Tabernacle located in the hidden back mountainside of Ishkooda where she worships Satan with heart and soul. The disciples of that church fasted and prayed wicked weekly prayers to break up marriages in the surrounding Christian churches. Also banning prayer in the school system was on top of their weekly agenda which they worked feverishly against. The Kingdom of Darkness was on high alert against the Christians in Ishkooda because back about twenty years ago a wicked team of evil spirits who had control over the whole city were banished, and exiled to an unknown destination by spiritual warfare. They had attacked the land, so there were no crops, no rain, and many murders.

All of this came about because one of the community's ancestors who once lived in there had committed mass murder. Over seven people were killed in a single household. The person was never caught by law enforcement, so the fearful story was passed down from generation to generation. But one of Sid's ancestor named Addie, took it upon herself to break the curse off the land. She was a woman of strong biblical conviction and prayer. Not only was she responsible for reversing the curse but she banished the reptilian face demons that had the assignment of the property, by sending them to the feet of Jesus for reassignment. This made the Kingdom of Darkness angry and vindictive.

So the little elderly lady from the Flea Market had carved, and made over a thousand shadow clocks which she sold from the flea market called sundials. She would always try to target lukewarm disobedient Christians as her primary customers. All the ones that purchased the sundial had no idea that the little old humpback lady had prayed wicked spells, and curses upon these shadow clocks which brought instant tragedy to their household once they got it home. The Babylonian sundial had a symbol on its face of the divine supernatural god called "Horus" which is the divine protector of the motherland. This is what summons the evil spirits to homes whenever they are taken from the flea market. The sundial was programmed by her demonically to operate counter-clockwise, cursing one's wealth, health, relationships, and children. She would always testify in the Satanic Worship Tabernacle that no one should have a god above her god. She served Lucifer wholeheartedly, the divine one. To overthrow the Christians through deception and mock the Most High, she would put the god, Horus, on anything she sold so they could give allegiance to her god. This was a violation of the Most High's law to have false idols in your possession.

There was an upscale, affluent gated community about seventy seven miles south of Ishkooda that made national news because of a mysterious sickness that struck all the children in the neighborhood. Their eyes changed to glossy black while their skin became zombie white with flesh eating maggots burrowing deep in the membranes of their flesh. An unseen portal positioned high above the heart of the community was maliciously open by a confederacy of six glaring red eyed angels called sun-gazers that flew through beams of light with thrumming wings scintillating against the sun with seraphic energy. As their heavenly celestial bodies were glistening like radiant white sparkling sapphire, they were airborne in the atmosphere on assignment to enforce a curse that was detected in the neighborhood. It was summer time, and all fruit trees that rely on self-pollination to reproduce were pregnant with juicy apricot plums while butterflies ballet danced in the ninety degree heat. Wild roses smelled citrus sweet while the lush paradise green grass was cotton soft to touch. Tutti-frutti scents of peonies and honey suckle vines stimulated their endorphins. As lasers of light penetrated the paradise neon blue sky, the curse was patrolling the community searching for healthy kids like predators to steal, kill, and destroy them all. A grip of fear paralyzed the neighborhood while overwork burnout physicians were making house calls, but they were unable to diagnose the no-name mystery disease. Ambulances were making roundtrips back and forth to the subdivision like starving vultures circling their near death prey. There stood the dreaded Angel of Death in his jet black goat-skin gothic robe at the entrance gate of the suburb that was responsible for the zombie epidemic. Three weeks ago a Neighborhood Association representative stopped by the community and had a device installed by a contractor right in the middle of the entrance gate. She was so proud of her investment because it added beauty to the wrought iron gate and community. She had no idea that the device that arrived in the mail was the cause of all the sickness and death in her community. It was gift wrapped in reindeer Christmas paper with a name tag attached to it that read, "Thanks for supporting our Church- Enjoy your Babylonian Sundial."

It was a mail order fulfilled by the little old humpback lady and the Satanic Worship Tabernacle from the dark magic dimension.

Summoning the Dead

After glancing down in her lukewarm cup of black coffee that supported her out of control caffeine addiction, she saw a reflection of her face staring back at her out of her cup while sitting crossed legged on a purple velour country style Queen Anne recliner in the heart of her dreary séance room. Zia had just finished chanting hallucinatory evil words in reverse better known as speaking in tongue backwards to summon her spiritual guide. She was trying to communicate with the human spirit of the dead for a client that wanted to contact her deceased lover who died eleven months ago in a drowning accident in the Okefenokee Swamp. The room was dark as a photography lab with thirteen lit candles burning like ribbons of flames around the antique table they were sitting at with an eerie, creepy feeling, surging and tingling up the visiting client's spine. Outside while the crickets chirped in unison like a quartet of violins, you could hear a flea infested stray hound dog lying on her front porch snoring with gnats covering his narcolepsy eyes.

Swoosh! Out went the candles as if someone sucked all the oxygen out of the room leaving trails of smoke from the candles due to the sudden outburst of dark energy with something manifesting itself from the mist of the smoke. "Did you see that? Did you see that," screamed the client, while holding her face with both hands as if she had toothaches throbbing on both jaws? "Shhhh," softly whispered Zia, while her client was confined to her chair with nerve shaking fear which paralyzed her emotionally. There appeared an apparition of a ghostly figure hovering in the doorway. The windowpanes begin to rattle while the champagne glass with a silver spoon in it by the tattered sofa begin to vibrate, sounding like an electronic chiming doorbell.

Fear flooded the whole room like the tentacles of phantom grey mist hovering voiceless and heartless while strangling it in silence. Suddenly there was a voice that fell in the silent room. You could hear nothing but the locust buzzing like electric shavers outside as the nightfall serenaded the daylight away. It was Zia's spiritual guide speaking to her with an urgent message of importance, summoning her for a meeting in the second heaven. While the spiritual chanting was taking place, Zia's client was smitten in delightful admiration as she looked at the Crystal ball surrounded by the hot melting candles. She could see her dead lover's face smiling at her as if he had never died. Then in a blink of an eye, darkness consumed the image in the crystal ball. The client yelled out real loud in a desperate voice, "Please bring him back! Please bring him back!" Zia responded by saying, "I am mentally exhausted! You must go, or you never will see your lover again. I know I sound real rude, but please understand." With an expression of anger and frustration, the client was surprised the way Zia turned cold on her all in a sudden. The customer didn't know that she and her spiritual guide was getting ready to go to an urgent meeting. The client pulled three hundred dollars from her pocket to pay Zia and stormed out of the house with her high heels shoes echoing with staccato taps against the hard wood floor.

Spiritual Espionage

"Have anyone heard anything about the case before the Divine Council," whispered Darfur with a calm energy to his confidantes in a serene tone while leaning back in his executive chair upstairs in his darkroom. Then one of his armor bearing demons that was assigned to him for eternal servanthood spoke in stuttering broken language reminding him that they were waiting on their best prosecuting team to get there so Satan's most experienced litigators can represent the kingdom of darkness. So Darfur, with bloodthirsty staring eyes began to smile with confidence because he knew Sid would be in for a vicious attack from the Kingdom of Satan for his violation of the Most High's holy word. The prosecuting team dispatched and assigned to the throne room was the legal team that's famous in the spiritual world for getting convictions on many Christian believers throughout the world. "Our dark angels are in a strategic position to strike him as soon as the judicial decision is rendered. Master, you are so excellent and wise. But the word is out in the physical realm that Sid knows his rule of engagement rights as a believer. He has sent many of our wicked angels reeling with undesirable flights to unknown places. He is skillful with the scriptures".

"Just shut up, screamed Darfur with gleaming eyes of malice! Just shut up! We got the little worm right where we want him this time. He will be the wood this time while we are the fire. Just like a rushing chariot of horses taking the enemy by surprise so shall our curses overtake him. We know the Old Testament just as well as he does so we now have convincing evidence showing him purchasing our little idols that are covered with spells. Those sundials are hot items, so we need to make the little elderly lady a millionaire. I have some plans for her and her grandchildren bloodline. In the meantime, I am reprogramming the lunar system because it's time base on the satanic calendar for some tragedies and natural disasters to take place according to our Schedule of Destruction. Bring me the list of all the weak believers in Ishkooda that are Praise Team Leaders. We got to attack some of their family members that are not covered by the blood of the Most High".

One December, a winter storm strangled and suffocated Ishkooda with a plague of zombie white snow. The nacreous moon freeze framed the holiday sky, as glowing fire flooded warm laminating heat from kettle stoves inside the myrrh scented homes. Red orange flames licked hungrily at the marshmallows being roasted over the glowing fireplace. Outside decorated pine trees flashed and flickered with dazzling blinking Christmas lights. Suddenly there appeared a young witch with sable black hair admiring a red brick home decorated with synchronizing and choreographing rainbow lights. Twelve giant red and white candy canes were staked in the crunchy cold ground surrounding the home where kids were building a huge snowman. One little girl suddenly threw a snowball and barely missed the witch's head then ran sniggling behind her friends playing in the snow. With fiery eyes full of rage and fury, the dangerous witch pointed at the candy canes and cursed the red stripes with magic enchantments. Suddenly twelve red snakes uncoiled from around the candy cane hissing with frosty fangs and slithered toward the screaming kids who ran and hid behind the snowman. After coming within three feet of the snowman, the red snakes mysteriously cease their attack and fled quickly from the kids, escaping in an icy pond. The kids were trembling and shaking in fear when their aunt came out to console them. They said the snowman saved our lives from the shiny red snakes. Then their auntie said, "Turn around and look behind the snowman." Standing behind the snowman was a giant warrior Angel with laser eyes glowing red, holding a flaming smoking sword over his head in a fighting stance with one foot forward and the other foot behind him ready to swing. All the kids fainted as the glorious Angel flew away. As of today, those white candy canes with no red stripes are still standing in the ground around the old dilapidated house.

Night Rider

A surveillance team of covert angelic Seraphim's assigned to protect certain houses in the neighboring district of Gaston, noticed a flying object approaching through the disguise of a thunderstorm north of their precinct. This object was traveling through the vast golden sky at the speed of light. A spirit guide was using the Windstream of the first heaven to time travel right up to the second heaven many light years away from the throne room where Sid vs. the Kingdom of Darkness court case was scheduled to start. The spirit guide disguised his mind reading signals from the holy angels that were assigned to the airspace. He needed to travel by using telepathy reflecting shortwave radio signals from a powerful roaming Principality Angel that protects roaming signals outside of their territory. The Principality, a beast of thunder and terror, would allow external signals to use his demonic towers for reception and transmission. Suddenly there was a burst of dark matter traveling at the speed of light right up to a designated waiting room in the second heaven. Astral traveling guest were forbidden in the throne room so they would reserve seats in the second heaven press room to receive updates from those that were subpoenaed.

Zia was suspended horizontally about six feet up in the air defying the laws of gravity through a demonic process called levitation. She levitated upward off the queen size brass bed in midair with a black velour blanket draping her body using pyramid power. Her feline eyes were closed while she was lying like a stiff corpse in a coffin where rigor mortis was full blown. Zia had compromise with the summoned spirit guide to use her soul like he had done so many times in the realm of the dead. The night before, she stood gazing at her Arabian giant crystal ball with the lights turned off in her séance room. Then she stretched her arms out toward the east and west with bleeding chopped chicken feet gripped tight in each hand. She knew the hidden secret on how to call up the dead to appear in the Arabian crystal ball because it was an open doorway portal to another dimension. She mumbled under her breath, "If I call the dead witch name, Miss Crenshaw three times into the Arabian crystal ball, then the evil angel will appear in the crystal ball before me." So she reluctantly began calling that name. She whispered, "Miss Crenshaw," once directly at the crystal ball reflecting her image while a scent of mystique floated in the air with blood dripping from the chicken feet spotting her floor. Then she slightly raised her voice saying, "Miss Crenshaw," a second time into the crystal ball but there was a mysterious animalistic sound that startled her. She said, "Oh, what's that sound?" It was nothing but her stomach growling from hunger. Finally, she screamed as loud as she could, "Miss Crenshaw!" for the third time while slinging her long black silky hair backwards like a heavy metal rock star. Suddenly a huge demonic shadowy beast with terrifying energy manifested and jumped out of the crystal ball diving into her soul. Zia, filled with demon power, screamed so loud until the heated crystal ball exploded like a grenade and shattered into thousand pieces of tiny glass particles, flying all over her séance room. She started violently foaming from the mouth while she rubbed the bloody chicken feet up and down her thighs. Outside her home, the ghostly magic was feeding the throbbing heart of the bewitching hour while wicked angels were attracted to the airspace above her home like green flies locating dead maggot infested carcasses. Her skin began to glow vampire white with a lifeless sheen while the demon wiggled his way down into her soul like a heavy woman struggling to fit into skinny blue jeans. Once inside her body, you could see a moving impression under her skin where the demon was slowly coiling around her spine like a serpent making his way up to her eye sockets to take control of her vision to enhance her eye gate. Then she began to have an out of body experience and started levitating as shadowy curls of demonic fire coiled around her diabolical body invisible to the naked eye. It was happening just like the spirit guide had promise. Her spirit and soul was separating from her body elevating into a higher realm appearing as a flying object. The Night angel activated her DNA for ascension through the fourth and fifth dimension to translate her soul to a higher traveling spiritual state in the twisted dark energy. Her eyes were a-flame with demon fire that caused a hair raising sensation in her body. Her body temperature dropped to near death level. There she was suspended in the air defying gravity like one riding on a flying magic carpet leased by a genie from a forbidden lantern. Her spirit was on its way to the headquarters of Satan in a vehicle called astral traveling right through the stratosphere arrangements the spiritual guide made with the Principality. While on her way to the second heaven in the star studded sky, she traveled over a particular neighborhood where believers had prayed for angelic protection. Up high in the atmosphere about forty thousand feet in altitude above the neighborhood, the airspace was controlled by the Third Heaven Angelic Air Force (the Most High angels) to enforce the prayer petition. These angels had received permission from the Most High to control all sky lanes and flight speeds throughout the heavenly airways over the neighborhood because of the supernatural petition. They also were given duties to scan the skies for uninvited wicked angels invading the protected airspace and to expel them by any means. Warrior angels monitored the air routes to keep the air traffic speed limit at the average light hour speed limit. The angels had a secret speed limit that outsiders were not aware of in the heavens, so if the limit was violated then a battle would be activated to apprehend all violator's like state troopers do in the earth realm. The sky lanes in the first heaven was like lanes on an interstate highway that was hidden from the naked human eye. Intercessory prayer protected and covered the neighborhood twenty four hours a day by summoning angelic assistance. Even though Ishkoodians stared at the measureless sea sky, they knew nothing was up there but clouds and birds fulfilling their destiny. Something miraculous happened several years back when the community of Ishkooda witness a fireball in the sky right above their neighborhood that was unexplainable. The mystery ocurred when two six winged angels saw an evil angel trespassing the protected airspace so they accelerated to speeds of 200,000 miles per second crisscrossing the target in a revolution circling cycle in less than three seconds incarcerating the demon, then changing him into a vortex of filthy dust, transferring him through portals to the condemned place of doom, called the black abyss.

Unseen cosmic creatures (angels) hidden in exalted heavenly altars would carjack falling stars (star-jacking), for a ride through the enemy airspace in the first heaven because most of the time the falling stars would be observed by divine angels as a dying star losing his position to a replacement star. Once the wicked angel saw he was past the warrior angel's airspace, then he would bail out of the falling shooting star like a pilot jumping from an airplane before it burn up and crashes at its programmed destination. When the evil angel gained illegal entrance in the new territory, he would clap his hands over his head three times then sparkling sheets of ultraviolet lights would surround him disguising his dark presence from the security forces of the Most High for ten seconds. During the ten seconds, he could fashion himself as an angel of light passing himself off as a 3rd Heaven Angel. These devils would try any trick to get around denied permission decisions by the Most High but eventually they would be apprehended by the Most High Angelic Air Force (the Most High's angels).

Zia astral traveling team had to take the long route away from the prayer protected airspace over the neighborhood before reaching her destination up in the second heaven.

Kairos Time

A sea of flowing electrons strategically set up their divine heavenly position in the strong electrostatic fields for building a strong magnetic force at the pole entrance for incoming guest. The Heavenly Council completed their divine meetings right before the east-gate was scheduled to open for the entrance of the Mighty Cherubim. The beasts of praises would follow this into a prepared throne room for an appeal by the Kingdom of Darkness against Sid. This Throne Room north of the east gate had been prepared to indoctrinate the judicial decision for the future case because other rooms were being processed for appeals on a lower court level. "Have you heard about our Majesty personally coming to this appeal because of the dark-side litigation team that just arrived"? This was the North gatekeeper Archangel speaking to a Council member that had just adjourned from an earlier confidential meeting. "Yes, I have heard, so get ready because we will have some action in court today, said the council member. His Majesty will still rule through his Kairos time even though he will display his omnipresence today." The Cherubim that's

hidden in the secret place of the Most High presence for roll

call was ready to commence the preliminary process of the

case by asking the Archangels to seal the throne room for the

immediate closing of the Northgate. For the Kingdom of

Darkness, litigation team had arrived with records, videos, and

sound bites of all the activity Sid had done over the last three

months. One of the Fallen Angels on the legal team name

was Saipon. He had brought in transcripts from historical

cases called Adam vs. Lucifer, Cain vs. Lucifer, David vs.

Lucifer, Achan vs. Lucifer, and Job vs. Satan. Through solid

understudy of millions of cases, they believe these references

would be the ones to bring a swift indictment against Sid by

nothing less than a conviction. Now all the Kingdom of

Darkness Angels came together in a football huddle to discuss

who would be granted the rights to present the opening

statement. The smaller burly bowlegged celestial angel pulled

out six straws. One straw was long, and the other five were

short. Then he whispered in a low delta tone pitch, "Whoever

draws the long straw from my hands will represent us and

make the opening statement. Do we all agree?" As he spoke,

he was beaming with confidence while he was looking around

at his team in the huddle. Then they all nodded their head. He

reached out to Saipon to draw first, but Saipon hesitated

before he pulled because he really wanted to get that long

straw. He desperately wanted to be the hero at the end of the

day when they win the court case by having the title as the

trial lawyer that brought Sid down. He closed his evil eyes

tightly and prayed to Satan for wicked favor then he reached

out grabbing the straw closer to him from the smaller demon's

hand. Then he open his snake like eyelids and saw the long

straw in his hand. A large smile lit up his face with the other

angels showing their approval because they believe that he

had the best experience in taking down Christians on this

level. "Order in this Court! Order in this Court", cried the

Bailiff Angel. "Please, everybody be seated." The evil angels

formed a single file line, Greek marching to their seats with

hands raised in the Baphomet sign showing allegiance to

Satan who was absent from this case. Then one of them said

to the other, "Where is the Creator of the Universe?" The other one said, "He is here, but you are not permitted to see him in his Glory fool! If we did, then we all would burn for sure before our time. This throne room was designed to accommodate us whenever we are requested to appear before him for disputes with his people." There was a jury comprised of Seventy Divine Council members. They all looked like angelic celestial beings with unique powers. It was time for court to commence. Sid was not aware that any of these events were taking place in the spiritual realm for him. But since he is an heir of the Most High and joint-heir with Son of the Most High, he was appointed a public defender automatically by the Heavenly court. Then two tall Seraphim angels with many beautiful celestial wings read scriptures from the text that Sid studied daily with glorious soprano voices. Finally they open the floor to the Kingdom of Darkness for opening statements. Saipon stood up boldly with a stack of evidence in his hands walking down past sparkling stones of fire in the center of the throne room. Then he began to speak in dark sentences lisping as he cleared his throat leaning forward with expanded wings revealing battle scars. The Angelic courtroom stenographer with nautical blue eyes starting typing and recording everything spoken, so a court transcript of the proceedings is created. "Your Honor I would like to address the court today by reminding everybody about a court case that took place many centuries ago. We all remember when rebellious Adam and Eve were on trial for sinning in the Garden. They tried to blame us for their Fall in the garden but to make a long story short; they were found guilty of disobeying the living word that came from the mouth of the Most High. We proved the fact that they were guilty by their words and actions. They were punished for their actions, and we were given rights to this world based on their transgression. They legally were cursed. Adam obeyed a woman over the Most High is really the naked truth." While he was speaking, his fellow comrades were leaning back in their executive seats with their hands clasped together behind their necks sniggling and nodding their heads at him showing approval for his presentation. They were extremely excited because Saipon was living up to his reputation for being vindictive.

While the court procedures were still in session, billions of light years away down below under the dark clouds in the 1st Heaven, a creature was slowly emerging, hiding beneath the ominous clouds with evil motives. The ghoul-grey mist sneakily hid its face like veils of steam lingering in the air after the rain. An Angel of the Most High caught his scent like a Bounty Hunter but there was nothing in the sorcerous sky to see. As the moaning wind disturbed the eerie tranquility, the creature peeped over the clouds again but quickly disappeared in the loitering insidious mist. After catching a glimpse of the illuminating red moon opposite the descending sun, the mountains casted long shadows of honey sheens over the towering trees in the valley below. It happened again! A silhouette of the thing slowly came in view but quickly vanished. The Angel saw something. Within the dark clouds there were glowing red eyes staring fiercely at him but the Angel dropped down low beneath the haunting clouds hiding himself from the thing. Then the thing began to slowly crawl upon the snarling wind with it shoulders low to the clouds like a lion stalking its prey. When he raised his head in the clouds

ANGELS FIGHTING DEMONS: Visions Through The Binoculars of Revelation

to spy the Angel again, he was gone. Finally the Angel sneaked upon the backside of the clouds and caught a glimpse of something huge hiding in the phantom-grey mist. The Angel slowly pulled his sword from his sheath hoovering quietly above him. Then he gradually raised his flaming sword above his head with deadly intentions beaming in his eyes. Suddenly he breathed heavily and didn't swing!!! Shockingly, there was a metallic skin Beast with six flaming eyes burning with malice, snapping his powerful mandible fang jaws in a show of force and intimidation. He was holding a messenger angel hostage in a tight bear hug with three arms. The messenger angel was carrying a prayer request for a dying child that needed an answer right away. Time was of an essence since the Beast had him in captivity for three days. Suddenly the Warrior Angel move quickly swinging his flaming sword at the beast face, which he blocked with his demon steel wrist band and blew fire at the Angel in retaliation. With all his might the Angel swung his sword viciously left and right at the weaving and bobbing Beast, but each time he blocked the blow with his demonic steel wrist band like a martial artist.

As the sky turned burglar black with thunder resonating in the air, the sword swinging angel finally thrusted his blade in the beast side causing him to squealed, breaking the sound barrier. The battle drunk Beast unfurled his colossal wings and escaped flying toward the east. With blinding speed, the Angel quickly caught him from behind and reared back to deliver the death blow but the cowardly beast let the messenger angel go and escape into infinity.

Preaching the Word

In the meantime down below in the physical realm where Sid lived, there was a revival taking place in Ishkooda about five miles from his home. There was a little old eccentric white church called the Upper Room. It sat between crowns of mountains in a valley surrounded by an old closed down petroleum plant that had many rusty fuel towers surrounding the whole community. It was a chilly evening with much precipitation falling causing everyone to scramble for their umbrellas. The rain sounded like buzzing angry bumble bees tapping on the roof of the car as the sky turned tar black. Stray dogs were running with abandonment for cover, trying to escape the wet torrential showers. "It's pouring down today," whispered one worshipper to another. "Oh yeah! It's that stinging rain too like biting flies. We better hurry up and get into the church". "Most definitely girl because I heard that the Pastor is going to let the prophetess from California preach the word today." "Say it ain't so girlfriend"! "Yes, it is my ace coon boon. The last time she came she prophesied and spoke into everybody's life with pinpoint accuracy." There was a line

all the way out to the streets waiting to enter the church.

Suddenly a late model sport's car with a screaming engine

sporting illegal black tinted windows, approached the side of

the church trying to parallel park. He killed his car engine by

turning the ignition switch off and stepped out of the car

jiggling his keys wearing a yellow pinstripe zoot suit, carrying

that old tattered torn bible in his hand. It was Sid. He fed the

parking meter and did a 180-degree turn toward the sidewalk

chewing a stick of bazooka gum while he was adjusting his

black satin tie pulling it knot tight around his silky white collar.

Upper Room was not his home church, but he was invited by

an old friend from high school to come and worship with them

today. He attended the School of Prophet's Church when he

was not visiting or doing his missionary work. When Sid

walked through the door with his hands clasped behind his

back, he looked and noticed all the seats were full. There was

standing room only. A year ago he had a strange experience,

when he sat in the congregation trying to praise, and worship

the Most High. The smell of spicy beef in fried onion gravy and creamy, buttery potatoes flooded the sanctuary from the adjacent kitchen with wafting scents of fat steaks, dribbling and splashing on sizzling hot oven foil, gave him a sensory overload. The scrumptious buffet smell filled the upper room sending his endorphins into orbit. The thought of food disturbed him so badly until he cried out, "How can a man worship the LORD under these circumstances."

It was about 2000 worshippers there trying to fill the 1500 seat capacity church. They were waiting to hear the rhema words from the Most High through the lips of the Californian Seer, named Sheba who was still mourning the death of her son, Bernard. Sheba had sunrise golden hair, strawberry-red lips with angelic Seer eyes that always had a pearl like sparkle and a curvaceous shape that many envied. But inwardly her spiritual eyes could detect like a cat scan, or x-ray machine when she gazed upon you. The Spirit of the Most High gave her the gift to see the invisible beyond the visible. Recently the Most High had translated her son's spirit from the earth realm to the third heaven by lifting him on the wings of a sparkling multicolored Cherubim angel flying him through the Pleaides constellation zipping him right into the presence of the Most High heavenly mass choir cheering his arrival. This glorious event was hidden from the natural eyes but witnessed by those known as the angelic watchers.

A tall usher half smiling with raised eyebrows dressed in a red, and white tuxedo, walked up to Sid with arms open pointing upstairs. Then he politely asked him, "Would you mind sitting up in the balcony sir"? Sid smiled and said, "No problem, I just want to be comfortable while the church service is ongoing." He was always conscious of his surroundings even in the house of the Lord because he knew that demons could transfer from certain people and attach themselves to others like blood sucking leeches. These people were better known as Satanic anointed carriers. Usually, whenever Sid sat by someone, they would gather up their belongings and immediately go find another pew. This was a mystery until he received a revelation on the matter. A year ago an oppressed backslider told him he fell under conviction when he sat by him and began to cry out for salvation because of Sid's anointing. While moving between the pews in the balcony, Sid finally found a seat between two old ladies which was the only one available. One of the ladies who had a beautiful smile had so much perfume sprayed on until it almost caused Sid to faint. He said under his breath with a case of mild throat constriction, "Now I see why this seat was available." By the time he sat down, the anointed choir had finished singing a rendition of "His eyes is on the Sparrow." Sid's guardian Angel took flight toward the ceiling of the church so he could sit on the crystal hanging chandelier to look down on the congregation for surveillance while the assigned angels of the other believers took up position over the air network above the church. Sid's angel didn't have to jump in the wind to rise from the ground for flight because he had divine high speed wings that gave him the ability to ascend, and descend with no effort. Each movement he made release afterglow sparkles, in snapshot sheets of lights that were only seen by chosen believers walking close with the Most High. He flapped his beating wings 186,000 times per second, in one wing beat which enabled him to accelerate light year speed. He also could stop on a dime after engaging speeds of 650 million miles per hour across the constellations. Aerodynamically he could maneuver, and make sharp U-turns in midair while controlling his body mass against any of the elements. Back in the day, some said this type of movement was responsible for summer breezes in the earth realm. Down below he saw a jutted face gargoyle angel with pitch black saber tooth fangs protruding from his mouth airborne over a guest visitor on the fifth pew close to the ministerial staff. This unseen guest was accompanying a soon to be exposed visitor. Warrior angels were on the scene like fighter jets flying low level speed monitoring the outside church grounds waiting for prayer warriors to command them into action. The angelic world was a myth to most believers in the Upper Room. Some didn't even know they existed.

Finally, it was time for the high voltage supernatural prophetess to fulfill her destiny by taking the stage. When she stood, the jubilant congregation stood screaming glory hallelujah with raised arms pointing toward the heavens. An explosion of thunder split the sky rumbling with rage as scintillating lightning flashed lustrous gold above the church. Darts of seething rain came spitting from the sky. Sid was getting overjoyed because he could feel the electricity in the air generated from the power of the Spirit of Truth which was moving in the midst of the people. Right below Sid in the pews close to the front of the church was someone he recognized, but he couldn't remember exactly where he saw this person. Then it dawned on him. It was the old humpback lady from the flea market sitting right in the midst of the congregation about five feet from the platform where the ministerial staff was. Sid didn't know that the little old humpback lady was a satanic worshipper, but he was in for a shocker today.

Before the prophetess started preaching, she told the crowd that she was receiving divine messages from the 3rd Heaven that there's a satanic worshipper in our midst. Everyone in the church began to look around at each other wondering whether it was the person they were sitting next to.

Then the prophetess had an open vision revealed to her instantaneously right in the pulpit from the Most High. In the open vision, she saw the little old humpback lady sitting in the front pew worshipping Satan with vipers coiled around her arms. (This was a vision Sheba was seeing in the Spirit that happened three weeks ago when the old lady was worshipping at the altar in the Satanic Tabernacle, but the Most High above revealed this to prophetess. Seers had the ability to see visions like watching movies.) Then she saw her making small sundials to put curses on them so she could sell them to the Most High people. (The Most High above was revealing again to the prophetess this woman's past.)

Once the heavenly vision ended, the prophetess grabbed the wireless microphone and told everybody about the vision the Most High had shown her. The congregation began to wonder who could be in love with Satan more than the Most High in their congregation. Then prophetess said, "Somebody in here is also selling curse idol sundials to the public from a flea market, and the Most High is displeased with you." Then with laser beam anointed rays streaming from her eyes face to face with the old woman, she said, "I bind the evil power of Satan that is empowering you to deceive the Most High people. Let every witchcraft curse break, be reverse, and disintegrate." Before she could finish her command, the old lady jumped off the pew like a wild kangaroo, grabbing her bags and ran down the aisle in fear of the holy anointing that was working against her.

She ran right past the deacons knocking down a little boy surfing the internet on his smart phone. Then she dashed through the church back doors fleeing like a shoplifter. But as she was running from the church, she dropped an object out of one of her bags. It was a Babylonian sundial similar to the one she had sold to Sid. The prophetess told the church the little old lady had prayed curses on the sundial so therefore it needed to be destroyed as the Most High commanded in his word. In the second pew on the left wing of the church was the association lady from the gated community twisting and turning her head searching to see what exit the evil old lady escaped through. When Sid saw the sundial on the church floor, his heart began to pound away in his chest like a bloodthirsty warrior beating a bass drum preparing for warfare. He knew right away he had one of those cursed items in his home under his bed. As soon as church gave benediction, Sid sped home driving like a thief in a stolen car. When he arrived home, he fumbled his keys on the ground struggling desperately to unlock his prison like burglar bar doors. Exotic fluttering moths were doing the electric dance around his bright golden porch light. Once inside, Sid peeled off his silky coat, running like an escaped convict toward his bedroom. He jumped and slid head first arms stretched out gliding under his bed like a baseball player stealing home plate. From the corner of his left eye, he noticed the skin on his forearm began to turn white as snow. Darfur legal team had channeled an encrypted signal to Demon-Freeze to time release the first stages of the curse the sundial was program to download. Sid ran outside searching for his can of gasoline in his garage. He tossed the cursed sundial on the ground then he poured gasoline on it. Then he ran back inside to get some matches to light the fire. There he was standing about six feet away from the cursed item ready to destroy it by burning it to ashes. Then Sid recited out real loud this declaration and decree. "I come against any spells, rituals, incantations, hexes, jinxes, sacrifices, and curses, raised up against me. Oh Lord, please cleanse the four elements, water, air, fire, and earth in my domain with the superior blood of your Son. Forgive me for harboring such a wicked idol in my area as part of my possessions. Wash and cleanse me in the name of Yeshua. I loose Giant warrior angels to fight and battle on my behalf. Every Satanic snare, penetration, and infiltration assigned against my spirit, soul, and body is arrested and blocked today. I overturn, overrule and overthrow it now. All curses are reverse in the name of the Most High". Then he struck the match on the side of his alligator skin shoe and tossed it on the sundial. All of a sudden there was a loud shrieking bloody scream blaspheming the name of the Most High coming from the blazing idol on fire. It was Demon-Freeze, the malevolent creature growling in the combustible heat, trying to escape the blood of the Most High and fire that was assigned for the destruction of the curse. Sid saw two raging eyes staring at him with an evil obsession in the dark mist rising from the fire in the shape of a three-headed serpent that sent chills down his spine like never before. Bellowing growls roared in the black cloud as it slowly vanished in the thin air. The curse was reversed and broken. Sid's flesh was healed instantaneously. Back two years ago the evil empire brought a case against him for practicing medicine illegally without a license because whoever he laid hands on was immediately healed when he prayed. The case was thrown out by the presiding Judge in the Third heaven.

Across town many miles from his home, the association lady from the gated community also had made her way back to the wrought iron gate. She hit her trunk release and got out of her sports car. Fuming with anger, she ran quickly searching her trunk for her tire iron. Once she found it, she slammed her trunk with uncontrollable emotion and purpose looking to get even with the empire of darkness.

She walked slowly to the gate like an experience western gunslinger ready for a duel. After placing the tire iron hook behind the sundial on the gate, she began to jerk, pull, and grunt repeatedly with no success. She fell to her knees like a defeated caged warrior and began to whisper a sincere prayer. Suddenly a homeless street person living outside the gates walked from the woods right up to where she was praying. When she finished praying, to her astonishment she had no idea that her answer to her prayer was a poverty stricken street person. She dropped all her wrong preconceived notions about the homeless she carried around for years by repenting immediately in her heart. This was an angel camouflaged in street garments that was sent to her assistance hidden from her senses and natural eyes. As he walked up to the lady, her heart began to race erratically with trepidation, then he reached out and touched her. There was an immediate transfer of miraculous superhuman energy from his right hand to hers. Astoundingly she felt new found strength in her body. She gathered herself up from the ground while grabbing the tire iron ripping the sundial from the wrought iron gate.

After turning around 180 degrees, her spiritual eyes were opened by the Most High. Then she immediately dropped to the ground falling like a dead man after looking upon the street person twice. The homeless man was gleaming and glowing like an explosion of billions of sparkling diamonds. He shot a stream of laser fire from his eyes as hot as a furnace at the sundial lying on the pavement in front of the wrought iron gate. Suddenly the sundial became a cremated pile of white ashes after hot beams of infrared, ultraviolet lights were triggered and blast from his eyes. His bone-white giant pristine wings were in attack mode as electrifying powers crackle through his skin like yellow spears of sunrays escaping through the clouds. His soul-piercing eyes scanned the cerulean blue sky with deadly intent. He was searching for gloomy evil hideaways in the raven-black clouds so he could jam satanic frequencies. This was accomplish by positioning his glistering anointed body in the path of the demonic engineered evil portal that was enforcing the curse. But his powers were restricted because of her lack of knowledge. He was waiting for her to give him orders to attack, but she had no clue about spiritual warfare and declarations. The angel withdrew and went back into undercover mode. If she had commanded him to fight, the battle for the gated community would have exploded in the heavens. So the howling messengers of death above the clouds were still able to reinforce the curse in the neighborhood because the lady was ignorant of spiritual warfare provisions and decrees.

Angelic Throne Room Verdict

Saipon, the evil angelic prosecutor, beaming with confidence, had just finished wrapping up his legal cross examination with Sid's guardian angel in the heavenly throne room. Then he glanced at his comrades with two cold eyes staring with an eerie foreboding, as he snorted whistling flames from his convex nostrils, above a goblin wicked grin smelling a soon to come 2nd heaven victory. They were high-fiving each other because they knew it was no way he could lose this court case even though Sid's attorney hadn't taken the stand. He knew he had proven his case beyond a reasonable shadow of doubt before the Supreme Superior Courts of all Courts. Then there was the sound of booming thunder and scintillating flashing lightning in the Throne Room. The court appointed representative for Sid was making his entrance from the Judge's chamber. Everybody in the whole Throne Room fell on their faces and bowed down while death like silence embodied the entire throne room. Even the evil angels with cracking molten like skin adorning their ossified bodies were prostrated and nervously trembling like sizzling polish sausages in hot grease. They were very familiar with this trial lawyer that made his entrance. This court appointed attorney was Sid's only beacon of hope to have his charges dismiss or acquitted. The heavenly Divine Constitution guaranteed him the right to have a court appointed attorney to defend him against the charges that were brought against him. The Seraphim and Escort Angels knew Sid was going to be vindicated when they saw one standing draped in a flowing white priestly robe as he majestically and gracefully walked in the midst of the throne room like a lamb slain before the foundation of this world with hair as white as snow; and his eyes were as a flame of fire. He turned to Saipon and said, "Vengeance is mine," then the post of the doors moved violently because of the rumbling echo of his cry, and miraculous smoke filled the chamber. "Sid is no longer in your hands because the charges against him have been dropped in the Judge's chamber after he repented under my blood sacrifice provision, so your permission has been denied." After he spoke, the Shekinah swirling smoke like glory begin to sparkle and vanish slowly away. Saipon and his wicked entourage had quickly exited the throne room court setting trembling behind the giant doors for shelter saying, "Everything is aching, my ethereal wings and entire body is screaming in pain because of that burning glory cloud." One greasy body satyr beast with goat horns adorning his scarred head said in a weeping voice, "My whole body is numb, I can't feel anything, and now my body is sleeping. Then the bailiff angel swung open the giant doors beckoning them with his massive hands to return to finish hearing the decision. Now it was time for the verdict to be read.

The Dark-side angels were traumatized by the glory cloud because of their arrogance that motivated them to sit too close to the public defender's table where the anointing was swirling around the public defender. This was the Son of the Most High representing Sid that was speaking. Then he said, "Sid has burned the cursed idol and asked for forgiveness. We have dropped the charges you brought against him today. Forget the plea bargaining. You do not have permission to attack him so move your forces away from him. Then restore back to him all stolen things you have taken. There was a loud uproar celebrating the decision by the all angels in attendance supporting Sid. Then a voice ranged out from above, "Order in this court, order in the court." A battalion of 3rd Heaven Bailiff Angels rushed the Throne room to enforce conduct codes in the Throne room.

So the disenchanted evil angels departed being escorted by a battalion of warrior angels to restore back all things taken from Sid doing the assault. In the meantime, Saipon delayed his return because he was appealing the case base on angelic due process of law. He was still arguing with a clerical angel saying he was entitled to a search warrant for Sid's house before the decision was rendered because the evidence was still under his bed. Since demons and wicked angels weren't omniscient, he was unaware that Sid had burnt the idol and repented of his actions. He was fighting a losing battle since Sid was protected by the best legal defense team in the history of creation.

Zia fell back on her bed after her spirit dropped back into her body from astral traveling with a severe headache swearing to never let Sid have any peace as long as she has breath in her body. The underground mumbling Chief devil, Canyon, with fireproof suede skin, called off the nefarious saber tooth demonic foot soldiers guarding the gateway tunnel to Sid's house. The Most High Third Heaven Angelic Air-Force were also dispatched to enforce the judicial court order. Toxic demonic gossip fumigated the corridors in the belly of the abyss because the word was out in the airwaves that some of the demons were upset about Sid's favorable court case decision. Some began to taunt the Angels from their hideouts, but they were no fools because the third heaven most skillful warriors had taken up positions in the first heaven to execute airstrikes. They were fierce fighters.

Conclusion

In the earth realm, after Sid had finished eating his lunch of crunchy peanut butter and grape jelly sandwich, the next day he went outside barefooted in his silky leopard skin pajamas to check his antique mailbox. He found a letter in the back of his mailbox sent to him first class with a free offer to win a brand new eight gigabyte touch screen laptop at a seafood store two miles down the road from his house. So he ran and jumped over a muddy puddle of water, racing up his concrete steps back inside his house to change clothes so he could drive down to the Fish market. His guardian Angel tailgated him flying gracefully forty miles an hour, twenty feet above him, with his doubled bladed sword unsheathed because he sensed demon anointing on the letter before Sid open it at his mailbox. Angels could see and detect devil DNA without any laboratory analysis because of their innate divinely created supernatural awareness and vision. While driving the bumpy back street to the Fish market, he hit a hidden pot hole in the asphalt road that shook his car like a light Alabamian earthquake. When he arrived, he saw from a distance a female vendor selling some raffle tickets to give buyers a chance to win a new laptop. After he got out of his car pushing through the crowd, his racing heart began to pound against his ribcage. He started experiencing the same emotions when he was at the Upper Room church with Sheba, as images of the past began to flash through his mind. You could discern unspoken words embedded deep in his eyes as his blood pressure rose to a danger level as he looked upon the vendor. It was the little old humpback lady! She made eye contact with Sid and immediately recognized him because of the anointing that was glowing upon his face like the setting sun. She said sheepishly under her breath, "It's him," with trembling lips and pumping adrenaline. The old lady began to shake uncontrollably with beads of sweat streaming down her peaches and cream, skin tight forehead. She quickly brushed the sweat from her forehead and bit her bottom lip to stop it from shaking. She had an urge to run and hide, but she started slowly stepping backwards. Suddenly, Sid's muscles in his stomach started closing in like tightening coils, as he screamed out vociferously at the old woman, "Stop"! Then empty silence sucked the life out of the atmosphere after Sid spoke, with his cheeks flaming with passionate anger. With an incomprehensible whim of fate, something spooked the patrons, and they all fled with terror as their hairs stood upon the back of their necks leaving Sid and the old lady alone to confront each other at the abandon Fish Market.

As the suspension of time begin to slow down to a nauseating crawl like oozing thick strawberry syrup, a shifting in the atmosphere started switching lanes in the soul black witch sky to bring the Heavens one step closer to Divine Intervention. The anvil shaped clouds were black as the devil's heart, casting dark shadows covering the ley lines on the ground below, where the Fish market was established which served as a gathering place for the evil spirit transportation system for demonic invasions. Sid along with other customers were lured into the devil's lair unknowingly disguised by a giveaway promotion program strategically designed by the master manipulator better known as Darfur, the lethal Ruler of

Darkness. He was power thirsty, dictatorial, hypercritical, physically violent, and domineering with an obsessive compulsive personality. The third and second heavens were counting down the minutes and moving closer to the first heaven to take up position in the airwaves for the next deadly battle just in case they were petitioned by their Ishkooda representatives. Sid represented the third heaven of the Most High while the mysterious old lady represented the second heaven where Satan ruled valiantly.

The Old lady raised her velvet eyebrows above her nebulous soul piercing eyes with a two tier ivory wedding veil covering her glowing face to hide her identity from those who cross her path. Sid's racing heart almost exploded after the old lady looked at him with her psychic star gazing eyes to give him the death stare for insulting her with a command to "Stop." She felt he had violated her personal space by coming too close to her proximity, so she threatened him with the old finger gun gesture. Sid hesitated before he responded, so he squeezed his eyes tightly shut and prayed a five second prayer under his breath for divine direction to the Most High as he slowly raised his hands above his head giving him praise.

When he open his eyes to respond, the old lady had disappeared. This was a mental mistake on his behalf when he closed his eyes to pray because he was always trained to watch and pray. "Where is she," cried Sid? A death-like silence blanketed the atmosphere while the sun shining like a gold medallion hid its face as drifting dark clouds began to drape the sky's ceiling blocking the peeping sunrays. Something quickly scooted across the parking lot that spooked him, so he quickly turned around looking from side to side and behind himself. He nervously licked his lips while gulping down saliva, then with a sigh of resignation he said, "The rustling leaves blown across the parking lot by the howling malicious wind sounded like footsteps." There was something creepy and mystifying taking place that was working against Sid which appeared to be someone working behind the scene to hurt him. He believe in putting himself in danger to save others so with a hurried pace he strutted up to the garbage dumpster by the Fish market searching for the old lady. He experienced cold chills tingling up and down his spine as he approached the dumpster. Then with both hands, he slowly raised the dumpster's lid. After catching a whiff of the rising putrid vapors, he quickly jumped back slamming the lid and fell awkwardly to the ground. He was hyperventilating uncontrollably while sitting on the grass holding his stomach tightly like a pregnant woman having light contractions. Then with both hands open, he began to fan the air toward his face to aid his breathing. He was hit by a powerful stench when he open the lid that sent him reeling to the ground like a punch drunk boxer. It was full of chopped dead fish heads and intestines that were several days old, shut air-tight in the sun baked trash bin that spontaneously created a powerful gas. Sid laid on the lush green grass by a tall spruce pine tree and fell asleep to rid himself of a painful headache. Suddenly he heard a cracking sound breaking the silence under the tree that startled him from his sleep. Then another cracking noise about a ten seconds interval away from the first one occurred again. Something strange started happening as if the noise was a warning sound preparing him for destiny. Twice dead pine combs and decaying twigs begin to trickle down from the spruce tree right around Sid as he sat motionless looking upward through the branches scanning for a stray animal hiding on a dead tree limb. When he jumped to his feet ready to run, there was an ear splitting cracking noise of a broken branch breaking loose from the huge tree that started plunging violently downward crashing and bumbling off the other tree limbs that became stuck on the last limb with long branches. One of the fork shaped branches had a woman's wig tangled up in the twigs. Sid squatted low to the ground with arms stretched outward, then he leaped up about thirty seven inches vertically and snatched the wig off the branch. When he landed on the ground, he noticed a pack of birth control pills that suddenly fell out of the tree. Then right above Sid, something somersaulted from the last tree limb and landed right in front of him before he snatched the pills off the ground. It was the little old lady! Sid was startled and began slowly backing up while trying to process in his mind what's the relationship between an old aged lady and birth control pills.

The little old lady shockingly revealed her secret after fate delivered her no other option by removing a big bulky polyester pillow from her back under her coat that appeared to be a hump. Since her wig got tangled up in the branches, she snatched the wedding veil off her face and placed her hands around the back of her neck loosening a tied knot; then she begin removing an old woman's rubber mask from over her head to reveal her true identity to him. Sid baby blue eyes began to swell with tears as he became nervously tongue tied while fumbling for words to speak after the old lady pulled off her mask. After taking several deep breaths, he began to regain some strength with his weakened voice and shouted with anger. "Zia"! "You foolish woman," while wiping running tears from his face! He was disturbed by the ungodly acts she committed against the Most High since they terminated their relationship. Then he said, "I knew an eighty year old looking woman didn't go around carrying birth controls pills for vitamins. You're on your way to hell"!

The old lady was Zia! She was living a double life to fulfill her destiny and purpose for Satan so she could destroy her former lover for rejecting her love. She had sworn to pay him back double for all the emotional trauma he had caused her, so the two spiritual warriors who knew the secret powers of the heavens were ready for spiritual warfare like never before.

Zia squinted her devilish green eyes while repeating an evil decree over and over again with both of her wicked hands covering her ears because she knew what was getting ready to happen when she stomp her left foot to activate the power of darkness. She was chanting an evil incantation petition to the demonic world to unleash a powerful curse upon Sid for intrusion into uninvited demonic territory. Then without any hesitation, she slowly raised her left leg from under her dirty ball room gown, while staring at Sid with zombie vision, and quickly she stomped the ground with her left foot, triggering the curse that disturbed the slumbering dead spirits below in the unseen underground world waiting for departure.

Like a popping wizard's whip, a bolt of lightning flickered across the abyss coven black sky releasing a burst of booming thunder eliminating the cocoon silence that caused Sid to hit the ground like a diving soldier dodging enemy gunfire. Zia, with drooling saliva dripping from her luscious lips, quickly grabbed a crooked twig from the ground and began drawing with the stick a pentagram in the loose dirt around herself in a circling motion so she could finish the second phase of the wicked curse. Sid raised his head out of the dusty red ground looking up toward the gun barrel black sky that was loaded with evil decrees from Zia programming the Sun, stars, and planets, to fight on her behalf. He turned toward Zia with flaming intense dilated eyes and said, "You're demon possess." She immediately cried out in pain because of his anointed words with a deep dark haunting voice hurling blasphemous insults at the Most High that angered Sid. The devil within was using her vocal cords to speak in stereo surround sound with a masculine bassline dark voice at 440 mhz. Dark misty like shadows manifested, twisting and undulating upwardly with the blinding speed of misbehaving wind shears gliding through the air like heat sinking missiles to prepare the atmosphere for the soon to come demonic angels. Sid's angel flew down from a thick branch high up in the spruce tree landing right over him dressed in full breast plated armor gear with his glittering sword unsheathed gripped tightly in both hands because he detected demon power in the cool misty air passing through the trees. The temperature dropped, and the smell of putrid septic gas grew stronger that made his angel aware that the approaching unclean foul spirits were coming to support the satanic angels for battle by preparing the oxygen and nitrogen in the airwaves for demonic warfare. Sid hopped to his feet because he sensed danger lurking in the atmosphere that could make the bravest of all soldiers skin crawl. Ghostly apparitions were surrounding Zia as the speedy demonic wind started twirling and swirling creating air pressure juggling the atoms around her feet activating levitation lifting her two feet off the ground.

Down below the cake crusty earth surface, the temperature increased as hot as four hundred degrees creating demonic convection currents that cause the earth plated mantles to shift, alarming burrowing hungry coyotes and carrion beetles to abandon decomposing carcasses which they were feeding on down in the bowels of the earth.

With a deep frown on his face and holy hands raised to the Most High, he began to counterattack Zia's curse with a tehillah praise. These praises prepared and anointed the nitrogen, oxygen, and gases in the atmosphere for holy angelic warfare that was conducive for angelic activity. Then he decreed with a loud voice full of faith, "Let a hedge of warrior angels surround me with Divine protection." He knew he was in the devil's territory so subconsciously he spoke to himself saying, "My battle is not with flesh and blood but with the power of darkness."

Sid's guardian angel took five paces to the right leaving scorched smoking footprints on the ground wherever his foot touch then he started in a circling motion taking fifteen paces around him and right out of thin air appeared twenty stunning gorgeous Top Model masculine Warrior Angels with wavy dark luscious long hair, halo white teeth, and muscularly ripped physiques, surrounding Sid with illuminating indestructible golden shields. They had irresistible dark eyes buried under their black thick eye brows with an angular, chiseled defined jaw line and cheekbone face with perfect unblemished skin. The Angels were sparkling brightly as if fistfuls of diamond dust had been sprinkled on their designer style priestly robes. They all were in an elegant fighting stance with their masculine right hands gripping their flaming anointed swords held high over their heads while interlocking their left hands together forming an angelic hedge of protection around Sid and speaking in mysterious angelic baritone tongues. What they were saying was a mystery, but it gave Sid strength and boldness even though he did not see them but he could sense their presence within the powerful barricade. The atmosphere within the hedge was sparkling as if the heavens had showered dream dust upon them as the Most High angels unfurled their glorious Super Turbo powerful wings. When the third heaven Warrior angels spread their majestic wings, it was an intentional warning gesture to the demonic world that an attack is imminent if the angels detect any aggressiveness from the evil empire. These handsome Angels were pleasing to look on but dangerous and deadly on a battlefield.

Suddenly a laser beam of demon fire hit the trunk of the legendary spruce tree like a straight line of silver lightning close to the hedge of angels protecting Sid. The tree bursted into flames with heat as hot as Satan's grill that barbecued and fried every branch on the spruce tree. It was a manipulative and calculating trick by the fast approaching fierce ivory eye demonic angels with horrendous color changing wings trying to lure the warrior angels away from Sid so they could smite him with a deadly disease for trespassing on their territory. But not one of the angels move with their unblinking laser eyes because their assignment was to shield and protect him by any means while he was on their territory.

Then Sid mumbled under his breath, "This Fish market must be Satan's Playground since the power of darkness is at its fullest strength." It hadn't been revealed to him prophetically that this was a recruiting center for Satan's kingdom, where

Zia and other disciples proselytize patrons that frequent the eatery. Once the candidate performed the evil confession and was converted to Satanism, then the restaurant would hire them mostly as waiters to serve their tables. Most of them would receive their tips from customers and toss the money into Satan's building treasury fund to finance future projects on their Satanic Calendar by taking a vow of poverty.

Once he realized he stumbled upon Satan's campground, he decided to leave, but Zia's heart started thudding erratically with a delicious fear because her appetite for a microwaveable warfare was about to reach its peak, so she jumped in front of him with extended arms and hands to block his path. "Get out of my way witch," cried Sid with an exasperated look! Then Zia disdainfully raised her hand in the Baphomet sign and spoke softly with deadly intent, "Make me." He refused to brush her off with a touch because of demonic transfer, so he quickly went around her looking behind himself every two seconds to deter a sneak attack by Zia. She couldn't see his hedge of protection, but suddenly there appeared a celestial fireball in the infinite sky which she caught a glimpse from the corner of her left feline eyes which brought a devilish smirk to her face. The kingdom of darkness called her dark beauty, the epitome of female evil. Then she silently motioned toward Sid with her right hand pointing toward the heavens. The celestial fireball exploded, resonating in the first heaven sky, releasing demonic dark angels like a vortex of hatred into battlefield formation, standing like winged barbarian gladiators in their dark glory on the shadowy triple thick clouds ready for attack.

Realms of dire black lights pulsated and menace in the sky like a deadly night shade, an undercover for the glossy black smooth skinned angels, to engage in stealth like ambushing attacks. There were many beasts grunting angels flying above the nightmare dark clouds, covering the daylight like a multitude of beady eyed ravens migrating toward their predetermined destination. The battle was imminent. The troll faced demonic angels with hollow, sunken red glaring eyes, and flesh tearing fangs were inspecting their surroundings to claim their territory over the expanded sky. Suddenly they began to echo an enchanting spell in dark unity on one accord saying, "Necropolis mutation! Necropolis mutation! As their sardonic smiles revealed rows of twisted needle like fangs, and a long thin, raspy tongue, with demon power escaping their flapping wings". They were numbered by their captain with a regiment of three hundred strong, ready to fight in the transparent (invisible) mode form so they could glorify Darfur, the Nemesis of the 3rd heaven.

Once Sid made it back to his vehicle off the satanic property being led by his flying angel, he said, "Enough is enough!!! I declare and decree, let the Mighty warrior angels fight on my behalf. Let the curse be reverse and backfire with double disgrace in the name of the Most High". Immediately the twenty Seraphim warrior angels with the looks of Top Male Models, disassemble the hedge of protection barrier around Sid with sounds of jangling and clanking armor. Then they release him back into the divine custody of his guardian angel. Sid was now under the divine hedge of protection fire wall provision, based on his obedience and submission to the Most High.

The twenty warrior angels with laser eyes stretched their flapping celestial wings in flight, and quicker than a flash of lightning they ascended with light speed acceleration, propelling themselves high above the marauding taunting devils, landing on a cluster of thunderstorm clouds facing toward the west. The silver lining of clouds felt like a soft bed of feathers under their light feet as they heat scanned with infrared laser eyes over a certain district of the second heaven for ambush attacks while on their surveillance mission before they engage the diabolical angels. The angels had the ability to see through electromagnetic spectrums, darkness, solid matters, and ultraviolet lights because their vision was designed by the Most High with secret light matter not revealed to humans.

The rules of engagement were received by the angelic team, so they switched from ultraviolet light mode to gamma ray mode that changed the DNA structure of their bodies. To change their celestial bodies to a fighting mode, the angels would cover their head and body with their colossal divine feathery wings, then open their flashing wings swiftly after rewriting their spiritual genetic codes which exploded like a bursting bright gamma ray revealing their new bodies. Their highly advance wings had the same matter embedded in their wings as the stones of fire along with clandestine secret powers that release recreating lights. Their Wings were weapons with recreating powers.

One of the Angels spied out a centauroid green eyed devil, covered with swollen tumors and crawling bugs, sporting a lion's mane full of golden wavy flea infested hair sitting on a gigantic flaming neutron star, wriggling his boa constrictor white-beige thick tail. He was assigned lookout duties by his satanic flying comrades, to alert them by demonic frequencies if back up squads were dispatch by the third heaven. The fuming Angel quickly snatched his sword from his sheath to smite him, but the angelic First Lieutenant read his body language, and darted toward him grabbing his arm to stop the blow, and said, "Shhhh, I have a better idea." He whispered to him saying, "We are obligated by the earth's domain rules where fights are regulated by permission's, so let's give them some of their own medicine they gave us last year." The warrior angel took flight like a supersonic fighter jet with turbo wings, dodging renegade meteorites right toward the moon through a lunar crater in a blink of an eye, then he close in toward the backside of the muscular centaur on the star, and blew anointed wave music into his ear. When the petrifying bizarre face centaur turned his Nephilim bulging head around, the warrior angel quickly hurled hot steamy moon dust into his feral eyes that sent him shrieking and flying blindly out of control through a black hole full of dark matter. "By the time he see his way out of the pool of black light, the battle over the Seafood district will be history," chuckled the Angelic First Lieutenant.

Once the secret surveillance mission was completed, the 3rd Heaven Angels turned their attention to the unseen wicked angels for unfinished business. The nirvana quiet mountains under the heavens below were draped with wintery covered snow like hanging white pearl necklaces as the earthy cologne of the sweet forest undulated upward in the ominous sky that was intercepted by a misty swirling smell of darkness.

The Leader of the 3rd Heaven angels equipped with the Lion of Judah tenacity, roared clamorously at the wicked angels as they descended boldly with their glistering heavenly bodies', right in the midst of their serried ranks inhaling a foul stench in the black nitro airwaves. He said, "Don't you horrible demons smell your own death in the sanctified wind? You have violated and assaulted our holy nostrils with your uncleanness".

They roared back in furious defiance, saying, "Bow down fools and worship us, or we'll eat your celestial flesh with Moses' manna for our communion"!

Uninvited Darfur glowing faintly in the twisted darkness, surprised all airborne surging beasts by ascending with a frightful energy from the second heaven. He came to lead and orchestrate the enchanting battle with his powerful warfare wings, covering his membrane torn muscular body. After bolting and flapping his wings, he glided in their midst surrounded by his shrieking fibrous potbelly imps, with tentacle tails that wriggle in the air behind their furry backs.

In a flicker of cloudy smoke, he raised his hand symbolizing the Baphomet with a bawling howl exploding from his gaping mouth in a show of force, then he yelled in unfathomable agony, "When you fight today, only fight over your territory." The nervous battalion of angels nodded their heads up and down reluctantly in the whispering wind, because back down memory lane, most of them that survived past battles with him in charge, had post-traumatic stress disorder after fighting relentlessly for him. The gossip out in the air was Darfur lacked leadership qualities to know when to surrender or flee when he's the commanding chief leading the battles. No sooner after he spoke, thunder tore through the sky as the whirling clouds turn into a heavenly theatre of death as he forcefully descended with a powerful gust of wind.

ANGELS FIGHTING DEMONS: Visions Through The Binoculars of Revelation

A crackle in the clouds, and a clamor in desolation, then all the elite Third heaven angels activated their second degree invisible mode to change their celestial bodies to deeper transparency and gradually disappeared like snow melting in the heat right before the flying devils glaring red eyes.

This ability of the angels to transform in many degrees of invisibility in different modes were unknown to the human race. Humans couldn't see them with their naked eyes, in their natural invisible form in the physical realm, but angels and demons saw each other naturally in the spiritual realm everyday, because of their supernatural binocular vision created by the Most High. Human only saw them through spiritual eyes which could be allowed by the Spirit of the Most High.

But there was a secret revealed as I saw the 3rd Heaven Angels with the ability to go deeper into another dimension of invisibility of another world, which not only hid them from humans but all demons too. This was called Twice Invisible. As shocking as this was, I had to take a moment to catch my breath. Hidden behind millions of sheets of lights, trillions of layers of the atmosphere, and million bars of unseen electrical grids, they roamed the 2nd Heaven free from demonic interference, and delays, because they activated their 2nd degree invisible mode (Twice Invisible). The higher class of wicked angels called archangels had the same ability too, but no lower class demonic angel could duplicate the feat.

Not a second later after a roar in the multitude of shadows, all the demonic creatures with diabolical restless bodies showing unimaginable force except for the lower level angels, transmuted their bodies by activating their second degree invisible body changer mode, which was still slightly visible to a certain degree to their rivals. There were several invisible modes they were equipped with that the naked human eye could not see. Their fallen state had damaged some of their fighting modes when they left their royal estate through rebellion. Some of the Ishkoodians called them light dimmers because after they fasted and prayed 40 days, they could see ghostly apparitions.

The devils didn't know the 3rd Heaven angels had a highly advance supernatural navigational system called Angelic Echo-location, where the shapes of surrounding spiritual beings hidden could be detected by them, when they sent pulses of sonograms into the airwaves, where the sound echoing in the air would reflect off the unseen angel's flesh that's recorded, and the displayed images of the invisible angel is produced. They were able to use this sonar radar to capture devils hidden in their 2nd invisible mode without bumping into them.

Plus divine intelligence had gifted them with the sharpest vision of all creation, where they could see through all demonic modes which the devils wasn't aware of, and hide themselves from all devils on all levels by going Thrice invisible. The flying devil's fallen state impaired many of their supernatural abilities.

In the earth realm, a group of locals in Ishkooda were gathered together in the street gossiping about seeing aliens up in the firmament of the sky over the last three hours, but a town drunk told them he started seeing angels after he stop drinking beer and start drinking moonshine. They all laughed and went home while the smelly town drunk staggered down the spooky asphalt road talking to himself with squeaky loud mismatch shoes on his feet. They didn't know; this man was a devil that morphed into human DNA form.

The pregnant dark moon shadow clouds full of sizzling electricity fuming with nitroglycerin like contractions, bursted forth into a liquid fire explosion sending unseen good and bad angels like shockwaves colliding against each other, as the Ishkoodian inhabitants below blame the shift in the weather on a fast approaching tropical storm.

Six shadowy smooth skinned dark angels with gigantic wings of fire moaned with rage as they twisted their elusive polychrome celestial bodies into a spinning action of sixty thousand revolutions per minute, then like six blazing arrows shot in different directions, they entered the first heaven sound waves hiding deceptively from the holy angels. Rushing mighty warrior angel's cladded in wind resistant white satin robes with blue steel like warfare wings stormed the boundless sky. Flying aerodynamically, they detected a legion of dark angels airborne latitudinal thirty four degrees, forty three minutes, and forty seconds north, with a longitudinal position of eighty six degrees, thirty five minutes, and nine seconds west. The unfathomable battalion of dark lion like angels wasn't aware the third heaven angel's had them lock on their bonfire red lasers. Then one of the devils with a crown of vipers wriggling on his head in delightful glee, looked at his black metal plated warfare robe and saw a pulsating red dot shining on himself. His darkest fear had come upon him. He shrieked and screamed desperately to warn the demonic air-force of the laser radar, but it was too late.

Angel fire struck they all!!!! An afterglow of a nebula radioactive molecular cloud rose in the heavens mingling with the elements, and slowly dissipated after an awesome display of explosive angelic firepower. The strong scent of burnt devil flesh gave the warrior angels a rush of adrenaline sending them into a frenzy of excitement, and ecstasy like bull sharks detecting delicious gourmet blood in the dark depths of the ocean. Their confidence grew, and their morale was high.

"We have been breached," screamed Darfur with the smell of burnt and roasted celestial flesh lingering in the air from the laser strike. "Return fire," he roared while flying covertly soaring behind his troops like a nervous night hawk for refuge as they advanced forward. "We see nothing," whispered the frustrated dark troll face angels who were beginning to suffer from claustrophobia, as they twisted their heads left and right repetitively looking for the hidden angels. The heat from the fire had scorched and charred their celestial backsides, which was like extra crispy fried gator skin. Fear paralyzed their wings for seconds before they could fly again, then the unexpected happened. Another laser burst of angel fire zipped through the air like lightning, clipping Darfur's underwings sending angel feathers flying all over the sky like a ticket tape parade.

"Ascend fifty degrees, fly thirty feet to your left then fire your lasers toward the eastern sun," cried the First Lieutenant to his battalion of warrior angels! He was motivated to spill their gaseous celestial blood. Suddenly a thundering Neutron star exploded! Star fire illuminated the virgin sky like a dazzling daystar baptizing the battleground with an engulfing suffocating heat with tongues of fire licking at the distorted face of the demons, offsetting their second degree invisible mode. Wounding their leader was a known fighting strategy of the 3rd Heaven Angelic Air-force, so their disciples would become discouraged and flee. "They can see us now," shouted Darfur to his troops!

The Third Heaven Angelic Air-force targeted the Neutron star for destruction, so the surprise explosion could frighten and lure the satanic dark aviators out of their hideouts, leading them right into their hands. After the explosion, they fled for cover, but they didn't see the 3rd Heaven Angelic Air-force with drawn swords ready to annihilate them.

Using their sonar radar, the warrior angels detected three silver potbelly demonic angels hiding and moving behind a force shield wall made from fifty sheets of radioactive ultraviolet lights, bonded with gravitational encrypted silent sound bars dipped in star dust. They ascended flying seven hundred feet high over the walls of the ultraviolet lights through tubular window chambers with their flaming double edge swords gripped tightly behind their backs. Then they tiptoed on the wings of the wind like ninja's right behind the potbelly behemoth demons, and quickly with both hands they ferociously plunge their swords upward into their round obese bellies. They twisted the blades with all their might by spinning their celestial bodies 360 degrees airborne and jerked their long swords outward by pulling it from their fat bellies that caused a popping erupting noise of splashing celestial bowels creating a slippery, greasy battleground in the heavenly sky. The troll face airborne devils were squealing and choking from their bubbling radioactive infrared intestines. A wellspring of blood sprouted into the air. For all their divine body parts were created from light matter which showed multicolored special effects when they were wounded. Their wounded bodies appeared like dark luminol clouds with enfolding fire flashing psychedelic amber lights blinking and sparkling intermittently.

Trails of rainbow like gases escaped in the vast sky swirling into infinity. The Ishkoodians meteorologist always wondered why red orange solar flares seem to be mixed in the dark clouds. The human eyes couldn't see some of the invisible wavelength of electromagnetic spectrums.

"We will not surrender," shouted Darfur to his troops after witnessing his armor bearers getting abused, and punished by the skillful angelic fighters! "They will pay for this coward assault on my dark elite soldiers," he said in a chilling trembling voice while healing a severe first degree burnt wound under his right wing with his ice cold fingers performing three dimensional dark magic. "I need a head count of all my wounded elite angels," barked Darfur to his Captains as the whistling wind beat against his feathery turbo wings. "We have the numbers for you already most unholy one," said a battle weary Captain. "Give me the digits," said Darfur? "Eighty one of our soldiers are wounded." Darfur, frowning with beaming brimstone red eyes, turned around 360 degrees in slow motion while flapping his wings in an undulating wavy motion caressing the wind giving all of his troops a death stare, then he said in an authoritative voice, "Everyone change your bodies to triple six cat-scan mirror mode"! "Master, that's illegal, and we can be banned or exile to everlasting darkness," whispered a wounded demonic angel nicknamed six o' clock shadow. He was responsible for assigning hindering spirits to block prayers at 6am in Ishkooda. "Shut up and obey my command fool, or be court martial tomorrow for trying to hinder me," yelled Darfur to the angel, seething with hot-blooded anger. Then shifting his thought process, he roared loudly to his troops in a baritone voice saying, "Everyone repeat after me, say darkness is beautiful, darkness is beautiful." The resurging legion of flying blasphemous angels raised their sparkling swords and began to chant in unison the secret diabolical black magic coded words. "Darkness is beautiful; darkness is beautiful," they chanted over and over again in the eerie echoing wind that summoned uncleaned spirits to saturate, and encrypt the atmosphere with dark power so that black magic could give birth to satanic miracles over the haunting territory. There were no portals over their fighting district so they couldn't summon more dark angels into the battle they were losing, so he decided to create a remote doorway portal opening by changing their bodies into mirrors for more demons to crossover into the battle. It was the same trick he taught Zia with the crystal ball. The more evil confessed in the earth realm by the Ishkoodians, strengthened the invisible empire presence in the firmament right above their territory which cursed their land. Then immediately the mind channeling dark angels activated their body change mode by covering their celestial bodies with their long gigantic wings where the magical powers were stored, then suddenly they quickly open their enchanting wings like retracting stage curtains revealing a multitude of reflecting mirrors of angelic bodies in the bitumen abyss black clouds. The shapeshifting morphing powers programmed in their huge wings, modified their DNA by rearranging their spiritual genetics with secret recreating lights emanating from their wings. Now, their mirrored bodies were doorway portals between both worlds. Immediately hordes of black demonic angels rushed forth out of the demonic mirrors, pouring into the infinite cursed sky like shadowy storms of locust darkening the clouds. This tactic was illegal and forbidden to use in this battle because 2nd heaven mirrors were doorway portals that allowed other evil angels to crossover into heavenly battles with no permission. But Darfur was so obsessive, and power hungry for fame until he was willing to risk his freedom as a rebel and be locked up in chains of darkness as a result of his illegal actions by the Most High.

Suddenly, cracking and bellowing thunder tore through the sky, rupturing the womb of the clouds that was churning with anger, leaving an aftershock that hummed in the air long after the rumbling noise faded away. The sky was boiling and roiling with a vortex of hatred. Writhing arcane lightning seared itself into a ball of fire, and scorched across the sky whipping the clouds with violence. The Most High was angry. When the Most High gave permission to Satan's angels to attack, the permission restrictions were recorded in the 3rd Heaven by his executive Cherubim Angels who archived it to the heavenly computer servers that outlined the start time, end time, type of weapons to use, who to attack, kinds of affliction, number of angels involved, where, when, how, and what time to report back to the 3rd Heaven. A warrant for Darfur's arrest was imminent.

Below on earth, Sid was relaxing in his vintage sports car playing anointed worshipping music through his fifteen inch subwoofers, while rendering intercessory prayer for the saints in Ishkooda. Suddenly it was revealed to him by the heavens that the territory surrounding the haunting Fish market was geometrically constructed on a blueprint of a pentagram. At each point of the wicked pentagram, the satanic worshippers had built a secret tabernacle giving allegiance to the most unholy one which casted a shadow of death over the entire region. The heavenly battle fought above by the angelic forces was directly over the Fish market that dwelled in warlock-black darkness. Zia only knew the secret behind the Fish market name and the Serpent Prophets, ordained by the Wicked Wizards of Ishkooda.

Zia was holding a crooked magic twig in her left hand made from Sequoia wood when she ran behind the Fish Market strolling through the wooded forest with dry acorns and wild nuts crunching under her feet that were scattered across the forest floor. Wild muscadine grapes were hanging from their vines like chandeliers with enchanting rubies. "I need more darkness, I need to go deeper in these woods so I can intercede to the power of darkness for our warlocks and sister witches that have infiltrated the local churches in the Magic city," said Zia. "For our satanic covenant protects us," she whispered. It was her set time for demonic prayer which was soon to come after she found the right location. She needed to perform dark invocations for the demonic angels fighting the third heaven so a boost could be given through her word curses because they were losing the battle. With the absence of the melancholy sunlight in the belly of the forest, the darkness shrouded the body of the woods like a black velour blanket. The skyscraping towering trees blocked the leaking daylight and served as a shady rooftop for the poisonous mushrooms, and hidden night critters. It was so dark until the only thing you could see was hybrid fireflies (lightning bugs) flashing their bright fluorescent bellies while shuffling noises under the decaying leaves intercepted the silence in the forest. Zia began to catch the glowing fireflies with her bare hands, with cat-like quickness, to perform illegal nature surgery on them so she could use their mutilated body parts for her final mystical and spellbinding act. From about twenty fireflies she amputated their glowing abdomen from their bodies with her fingers, so she could mark her four entry gates on her face for spiritual marking. "Wow these things stink," said Zia after getting a whiff of the foul smell emanating from her stinky fingers. Her eye gate, mind gate, ear gate, and mouth gate were engaged for spiritual contact with the dead.

The Ishkooda darkness was so thick in the forest until one could almost slice it with a knife. In the lagoon blackness, she attached a glowing firefly belly on each of her ears, one on her forehead, one over each eye and fifteen of them around her mouth. The firefly earring was glowing on her ears like sparkling diamonds in the darkness along with the flashing bellies on her forehead, eye lids, and mouth. Her head looked like a bootleg jack-o-lantern Halloween pumpkin. Using her magic wand, the crooked twig was leading her like a GPS device in the thick darkness. Finally, she was able to locate an old ancient tombstone without any source of light. She needed a corpse or decompose body for her necromancy moment.

As the wind exhaled, she took the glowing firefly bellies from around her mouth and rubbed her hands together smearing them all over her palms. Her hands were glowing in the dark against the Beelzebub blackness from the smeared firefly bellies. "This is an isolated spot for me to invoke my chants to the power of darkness," Zia said while standing in front of the vaulted tombstone with twisted arthritic honeysuckle vines covering its entire surface. "I wonder who is buried in this vault," she softly whispered to herself. She raised her hands up toward the tombstone and the glowing light shined from her hands on the faceplate of the tombstone in the surrounding darkness. What she saw next was horrifying. Her eyes became wide as saucers with her mouth dropped open. She screamed at the top of her lungs, awakening the evil spirits in the sleepy airwaves. Her piercing screeching voice echoed all the way from the raging womb of the forest to its outskirts. Zia, with bulging eyes, raised both arms up in the air to use her glowing dripping fluorescent hands as headlights against the darkness, while walking backwards slowly, and then suddenly she turned around running as fast as she could back out of the spooky forest, slipping, and sliding on the damp swampy forest floor trying to escape. She was startled when she shined her glowing hands on the tomb, and saw an indigent dirt poor street person with flaming eyes, standing bowlegged on top of the tomb, pointing a shiny cross in front of her face that frightened her almost to death. The street person was the same undercover angel that came out of the woods and assisted the neighborhood association representative at the gated community. Suddenly Zia's hidden amphibious disembodied foot soldiers who were assigned to protect her through satanic covenant provisions immediately swung into action. As silent vines dangled from sprawling trees, three crawling deformed gigantic beasts with glaring hypnotizing swirling eyes, was incense with a burning rage. They urgently advanced forward with a terrorizing energy from the ossuaries where the lower level infantry ground forces with supernatural foot speed, and night vision hid in a subterranean hideout feeding secretly on the dead in subzero temperatures. They quickly surrounded the vaulted catacomb tomb with their basilisk dilating eyes, and snarled at him. After menacing with their barracuda mouth full of needle like fangs, they barked in a beastly grunt saying, "How much power do you have"? The calm and cool celestial warrior held his peace because he had receive permission to protect the remains buried in the vaulted tomb by the 3rd Heaven. The bizarre beast gazing with a wicked furor didn't know that intercessory prayer by the Assembly Apostolic church for protecting the land, had ushered him in their presence. The bones in the casket belonged to an anointed fire and brimstone preacher name Pastor Jeremiah Goodfoot who performed numerous miracles in many Ishkooda tent revivals. The Angel was there to stop Zia from robbing the grave of body parts for her next ritual.

As sparkles exploded from their tusk mouths, violent flames, and smoke rose from their twisting nostrils as they were ready to lunge forward to attack, until the demonic leader of the assault team said, "Cease fire." With swooping tree limbs casting eerie shadows below, intense heat begin to escape his mouth as the devil sensed angel DNA emanating from the impoverished man causing him to tremble and shake uncontrollably. He realized this was a high ranking Seraphim who was extremely dangerous under disguise, fully loaded with destructive fire power. Quickly he hissed a whistling snort from his wolf like nostrils warning his troops. A sunken face demon with scythe like glowing bones, and see through membranes, screamed at the leader saying, "Lets launch the arrows before he hit us," as the blaring echo resonated from his rigid mouth. He reached out his frigid hand touching the indigent man foot with threatening energy, but he withdrew his hand quickly noticing that he was burnt. This angel was too hot for them to handle. The undercover angel patience was running out after tolerating all the taunting from the bony headed demons, and suddenly he raised his hands to the sky saying, "All Praise to the Most High, in the name of Yeshua I will drive this darkness back to the abyss." He was ready for war. The confused demons looked at each other speechless. When the Third Heaven angel spoke, it was in an unknown mysterious angelic tongue confusing the imps. Then his splendid, glorious warfare wings, with light speed ability, unfurled miraculously from his muscular celestial back covering the entire circumference of the battleground right before the eyes of the demonic blood sucking troops. Pools of dark shadows lurking over the showdown began to dissipate as a brigade of insects swirled over the spellbound territory. His body heated up to about fifteen hundred combustible degrees to warfare temperature, consuming his street garments, and sandals revealing his varnish clear Corinthian shoulders under his heat resistant Ephesian robe, with a white marble like muscular physique revealing a rippling washboard iron like stomach. His sun like presence chased the forest darkness away. Everything was naked before the daylight eyes.

He gave the demons the death stare, jumping down off the tomb, with his right hand gripping his supernatural sword, landing flat foot in the death pit face to face with the nightwalkers. The Angel glanced at the forest floor and saw hundreds of goldenrod-yellow flowers scattering pollen on the ground like spicy mustard powder. With his glorious wings beating against the eerie night wind, clouds of pollen dust was stirred up from the forest floor, camouflaging him in a dense blanket of yellow fog. He intentionally stirred up the pollen dust to conceal himself from the demons because of his glistering brightness. When the vaporous pollen mixed with swamp dust dissipated, the Angel vanished from within the circle of the demonic foot soldiers.

The snarling demons, standing with hands on their hips with sharp daggers hanging in their sheath from their thighs, shaking their thick lion like manes vigorously with darting red eyes searched for the missing Angel. "All troops withdraw now," cried the gaunt face demon after witnessing the dramatics of the anonymous angel. "Where is he," whispered the confused demons? This was an unseen battle hidden in the natural which only could be witness in the spiritual. The rules of engagement for the battle was ground techniques, but no aerial assaults were permitted. Since this was the earth domain they could not utilize all of their weaponry, and spiritual form without heavenly permissions in this battle. They had to fight this battle in limited human form downscaling their angelic powers. In a clamor of beastly noises, demonic spirits with sounds of roaring fire escaping their draconic nostrils scanned the towering sycamore trees with their night vision encapsulated eyes, searching for the Angel whereabouts as they began to disband. Some began to celebrate the disappearance of the Angel as a victory for Zia by planning for a night raid on four Ishkooda families that bought idol worshipping dolls from a thrift store. One of the families targeted was the son of a Bishop that was the church organist and choir director.

But it was too late. The determine Angel was hiding inside the sealed vault tombstone with no cabin pressure below the casket, listening attentively to the demonic plans outside, right before he slid the vaulted lid aside just enough to crawl out for a surprise attack. He quickly soared twenty feet high into the air with his flaming eyes on the Alpha beast as his target. He landed behind the disassembling troops ready to strike, but he forgot about the hot devil spit better known as poltergeist white misty stardust, escaping into the atmosphere. Alarming vibrations and frequencies from demonic tracking devices went off warning the demons of a trespasser. The 3RD Heaven Angel swung at the bulging face demon with a loud grunt as the devil leaned backwards like a surfer on a wave, with the malicious sword missing him by centimeters. The probosci's nostril beast felt the passing wind from the swishing sword that left a small gash on his steel plated neck. Breathing heavily with a rush of adrenaline, the Angel did a double sweeping swing with his sword clenched tightly in his fist by returning a second death blow in the opposite direction toward the frighten demon, but he leaped five feet high barely escaping the slicing blow. His strategy was to destroy the Alpha demon so he could discourage the others to flee. "Their hot devil spit is the hidden tracking device that threw me off balance," whispered the Angel.

His plans backfired! Six staring zombie eye demons with curved tusk protruding from their hollow mouths separated from the pack, and began to beg the Angel to fight them with a come here curled finger gesture. With squirming high voltage tentacles adorning their heads, they had obsidian black gangrene skin with flesh eating worms churning and wriggling in their wet creamy transparent bellies. You could see squirting fat overfed slimy maggots squirming in and out between their teeth feeding on leftover human flesh. They were grave hunters by night feasting on endoskeleton soft tissue from cadavers as a delicacy in the sleepy soul of the thicket. With the shady skyscraping trees staring below, and the sun hiding his face over the glossy black Ishkooda sky, the battle began to intensify. Warrior Angels on assignment covering the airspace over some local homes just a few miles away, heard from other messenger angels that a battle was taking place in the woods, which drew their interest. But these

Angels could not assist because they were on strict assignment to stay with their subjects.

The menacing infernal demons with red hot stubby horns, reared back like a pitcher, and fired their somersaulting deadly daggers in the air, zipping like lightning just missing the invincible Angel, as he quickly dived in a swampy pool of mosquito infested water, escaping the lethal daggers. Bewailing noises ghosted through the trees as steamy purified water vapor escaped toward the boundless sky from the ground as his sizzling hot glossy body laid in the evaporated pool like a misdirected ballistic missile. The irritated Angel became extremely angry with thoughts of burning the whole forest down. This Angel was from the ranks where they fiercely defended their territory with dangerous firepower. So while on the ground he positioned himself in a sitting position, then he began to flap his torqueing wings in a downward motion behind the passing daggers, and the powerful downdraft air increase to hurricane wind force strength causing the daggers to boomerang swiftly back at the demons. The terrified hairy demons with a pair of scaly gargoyle wings furled up behind their back, ran as quick as the eye can see, dodging the weapons. The swords hit a dead decomposing oak tree with beards of hanging moss with so much force, until it was torn asunder. "Return to Sender," said the Angel as he rose to his feet shaking the dust from his wings. He began to repeatedly nod his head up and down, while staring at the confused demons that were stepping backwards slowly with compact, muscular legs, as he sarcastically said to them, "Stop trembling." He finally decided to end the chess minded battle by striking all the imps with blindness. He caught the snarling wind in both transparent fists and withdrew all of the moisture from the cold air by inhaling it through his divine nostrils, changing its composition while increasing the atmospheric pressure, then he clapped his hands at the imps blinding them all when he exhaled. The blind demons knew the dark back woods like humans know their houses when they lose electrical power. They mysteriously return to their underground headquarters for recovery like misty shadows of vapor.

ANGELS FIGHTING DEMONS: Visions Through The Binoculars of Revelation

Zia had found her way out of the maze like dark forest while rushing back up to the Fish market to see whether Sid was still sitting in his car. A police cruiser with flashing blue lights was sitting next to Sid's car, but he was nowhere in sight. Someone had called the cops, and he was shining a halogen flashlight around the burnt spruce tree looking for evidence. He was also writing a report on vandalism and destruction of property. Zia was peeping around the corner of the Fish Market dumpster hiding from the police because she recognized Sid was sitting in the back seat of the cop's car. "Mama's baby is on his way to jail," she whispered to herself while sniggling under her breath. "So much for the saying, the righteous shall prevail," she said while laughing to herself and holding her hideout position behind the putrid dumpster.

In the meantime, a funeral procession with many cars leading the line was making its way down the road past the Fish Market with a large twenty four karat gold plated coffin on the back of a white carriage being transported by a team of Clydesdale horses.

Up under the street light, Zia's shadow was pantomiming back and forth behind the dumpster, which Sid noticed while sitting in the police car. When Zia peeped again around the dumpster, Sid saw her and got the cop's attention by pointing his nervous finger at Zia through the police car window saying, "There she is"!

After realizing she had been snitched on by Sid, she bolted from behind the dumpster rushing into the edge of the woods stumbling over pine combs, running to the other side street where the funeral procession was traveling. The Cop gave chase through the creepy woods, but he lost track of her, so he return to the car. He got back in his vehicle and left the Fish Market traveling in the left lane passing the funeral procession with Sid still in the back seat. Sid was twisting his head left and the right looking out the window for Zia but she had disappeared in the thin air. As the car approached the Clydesdale horses transporting the deceased, the coffin door lid mysteriously cracked open an inch. A pair of feline eyes were peeping at Sid from inside the coffin as the patrol car pass the carriage at a slow speed. It was Zia laying on top of the dead body in the closed casket with squinting eyes peeping at Sid. Earlier when she ran through the dark forest out to the side street, she ran behind the high stepping horses then climbed the carriage and opened the coffin to jump inside laying on the dead man so that she could hide from the pursuing police.

The beer breath coachman sitting in the carriage smart phone started ringing. The caller wanted to know what time the body was going to arrive, so he could have the chamber ready. The coachman spoke with a slurred voice saying, "We are already outside in front of the building." The name on the sign in front of the building on Judgement Blvd was Ishkooda Crematory. The inebriated coachman reached back behind his seat and hit the lock on the casket then started helping others to carry the coffin inside to prepare the decease for cremation. The nickname of the deceased man was Mala Suerte which means bad luck in English. When he was alive, everyone that came in contact with him seemed to fall under a deadly curse.

In the meantime, the Cop that was transporting Sid in his unmarked patrol car didn't take him to the local jail, but instead, he was pulling up in front of Sid's house to let him out. Sid guardian angel was standing on the rooftop of his house rubbing his chin with his angelic fingers, wondering why he was detecting Angelic DNA coming from the patrol car. When Sid stepped out the car, he held his head back through the window with his hands in his pockets, and said, "What's your name officer"? The officer turned toward Sid with sparkling eyes, replying, "Just call me First Lieutenant." Sid smiled and waved goodbye as the angel drove out of sight. Sid didn't know the policeman was an undercover 3rd Heaven First Lieutenant Angel that was fighting Darfur and his mirror reflecting angels in the heavens, which was still ongoing.

On Judgement Blvd, thick coiling black smoke rose into the infinite sky from incinerator smoke stacks over the crematory which left a smell of human remains in the atmosphere. Did fate deliver Zia her final act?

It's about 3:00 a.m. in the bottomless depths of Hades where the smell of oven burnt flesh flooded the place, while velvet black demons river dance with hands on their hips, in the scorching red hot lava fire. When the demons finished dancing, they began to chant and hum in unison on a low frequency. The dynamics of the frequency sound they were chanting, unlocked six encrypted doorway portals in the second heaven which release galactic cosmic rays that showered the earth atmosphere with twisted dark energy. There was bellowing in the depths of the bowels of Hades under five layers of darkness full of chaotic energy. Hidden secret passages led to an underground Giant gate with huge metal doors where a draw bridge was being lowered for thousands of demonic troops to crossover. They were being called up from the Satanic Military Reserve for upcoming battles to be fought in the 1st and 2nd Heavens. Warfare prayers were taught in Sunday school in Ishkooda, and Warriors angels from the 3rd Heaven were on their way to battle evil angels in the 2nd Heaven because of these prayers. Darfur's 2nd Lieutenant made a declaration throughout the

ANGELS FIGHTING DEMONS: Visions Through The Binoculars of Revelation

territory requiring all devils in Ishkooda to enroll in Satan's Selective Service Draft because of these prayers. They posted Most Wanted posters of intercessors in the small town, and a bounty was placed on their heads. It was open season on all prayer warriors. Hit squads and contracts were signed in darkness to spill innocent blood by Secret infiltrators. A new battle was brewing on the horizon as Sid prayed the 91st Psalms before going to bed with a Giant angel standing and glowing in his doorway.

ANGELS FIGHTING DEMONS:

Visions Through The Binoculars of Revelation

Demons are legalist which is why we need to be experts when it comes to the written laws of the Most High. When Sid transgressed the Most High's law, the legion of devils were ready to point it out to the Most High so they could receive permission to attack him. When you are out of fellowship with Jehovah-Shalom, the enemy can launch attacks and enter the breach in your hedge of protection to bring evil tidings. Sid was able to restore fellowship before the enemy completed their assignments. Thank God for Grace. Sid knew his rights, but Satan had a trick he downloaded to the mind of the old lady that was causing nightmares for many believers. Sid escaped the trap, but the Old Lady is back at it again. What's her next move? The Angels battle Demons to protect Sid after he requested divine assistance in spiritual warfare where conflict after conflict loaded with action pack tactics will leave you in suspense wondering who will be on the winning side.

ANGELS FIGHTING DEMONS: Visions Through The Binoculars of Revelation

Seeing Through the Binoculars of Revelation

And Elisha prayed, and said, LORD, I pray thee, open his eyes, that he may see. And the LORD opened the eyes of the young man; and he saw: and, behold, the mountain was full of horses and chariots of fire round about Elisha.

1st King 6:17

King James Version

By Author

Milton Epting

Jesus is Lord

SID VS. THE KINGDOM OF DARKNESS